IN THE
SHADOW
OF THE
WOLF
QUEEN

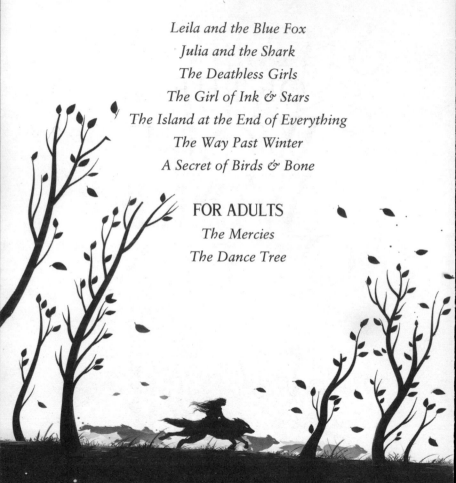

KIRAN MILLWOOD HARGRAVE

IN THE
SHADOW
OF THE
WOLF
QUEEN

A GEOMANCER BOOK

Orion

ORION CHILDREN'S BOOKS

First published in Great Britain in 2023 by Hodder & Stoughton

This paperback edition first published in 2024

1 3 5 7 9 10 8 6 4 2

Text copyright © Kiran Millwood Hargrave, 2023

Illustrations copyright © Manuel Šumberac, 2023

The moral right of the author has been asserted.

A CIP catalogue record for this book is available from the British Library.

ISBN 978 1 510 10785 4

Typeset in Sabon by Avon DataSet Ltd, Alcester, Warwickshire

Printed and bound in Great Britain by Clays Ltd, Elcograf S.p.A.

The paper and board used in this book are made from wood
from responsible sources.

Orion Children's Books
An imprint of
Hachette Children's Group
Part of Hodder & Stoughton Limited
Carmelite House
50 Victoria Embankment
London EC4Y 0DZ

An Hachette UK Companywww.hachette.co.uk

www.hachettechildrens.co.uk

For our daughter,
the start of my greatest adventure

BOOK ONE:

IN THE SHADOW OF THE WOLF QUEEN

*'Perhaps the tips of trees
are roots that drink the skies'*

from *Orchards* by Rainer Maria Rilke (translated)

*'But there is a long way to go before then,
and the path takes many turns.
It begins at the trunk of a tree'*

from *The Children of Ash and Elm* by Neil Price

Wakening

It woke the world the way wind wakes air.

Where once things were still, now they stirred. The trees of Glaw Wood took up a lazy swaying, straining their roots as if to walk. The birds took off from the branches and made shapes like flung silk in the sky, and in the mulch of the cool, wet dirt the ants trailed determinedly away.

In the cold salt-and-darkness of the Tarath Seas the whales heaved their bodies from the waves, the sharks sank to the seabed, and the stingrays flew from the water, bodies like spinning blades. In the cloud-strewn Drakken Peaks, the earth-old rocks rippled like water and shook the snow from their summits. Beneath the tidal heave and pull of the hidden meridian, in the halls of the dead the spirits paced like caged tigers, rootless.

In a castle built of broken boats, a wolf queen sharpened her spear. In the hall that was once his fortress, a rebel lord buried his wife. In the mountains, an ancient girl opened her cobwebbed eye, and flexed her stone-clad fingers with sounds like dropped pebbles.

The earth music had begun, and they must make ready.

CHAPTER ONE

SNARE

'Nara, hush!'

The forest was speaking. Beneath the deep copper fire of the Elder Alder, Ysolda sat cross-legged on the ground, and tried to listen. To her heart she pressed an amber amulet, worn smooth and orange as flame by constant touch, and her feet were bare and buried in moss. Nara was flying a wide loop above her head, and somewhere to the left a sparrow was calling a warning to its mate as the sea hawk swooped her circle.

'Hush, Nara,' hissed Ysolda, glaring through a half-closed lid.

The hawk snapped her beak as she glided past, cuffing Ysolda's cheek lightly with her speckled feathers, but obeyed. She knew not to make a fuss when Ysolda was attempting to listen.

Ysolda closed her eye again and pressed the amulet tighter to her chest. She tried to block out Nara's huffy chitter, the sparrow's continued panic, and focused on the forest again, straining to hear the water below her, the trees sharing space and eras, passing knowledge between them like blood. Hari said it was all there, all the time.

They're not speaking words. You can put our words to what they say – 'follow', 'down', 'here' – but they don't reach for what is actually meant. It's instinct that truly passes through you when you're listening, a feeling. Words aren't enough, like 'hunger', like 'love'. They fall short. You don't have to be special to hear: you only have to listen.

It was easy for her to say, with her luminous skin and bronze eyes. Ysolda knew better than to judge by appearances, but if anyone were asked to imagine what a special person who could hear trees looked like, they would think of someone like Hari. So when her sister said listening could be learned, Ysolda didn't really believe her.

Crunch. Crunch.

Ysolda cracked her eyelid again. Nara sat atop a mossy branch, having skewered a large black beetle with one nail-length talon. She was now pulling its legs off one by one and staring back at Ysolda as she did so, clicking her beak insolently.

'Sea hawks aren't meant to eat beetles,' said Ysolda.

Nara bit off another leg.

Ysolda rolled her shoulders, blew out a short, impatient breath, and tried to retreat once more into the place Hari had described, where your body was only air and listening. If she was going to hear it anywhere, it would be here – beneath the first tree that began their forest, and where all the words of Ogham, the language of trees, were inscribed – with Hari's amber amulet pressed against her heart. But now her neck was aching, and her stomach was rumbling, and her leg had gone to sleep.

She threw the amulet from her with a frustrated little shout. 'I almost had it there! If you hadn't scared that sparrow—'

Nara's feathers ruffled, and Ysolda's anger went out of her. She sighed, and slumped back on the springy ground. It was damp, as always. In Glaw Wood, if it wasn't raining, you were inside. It's what gave the place its fierce green, so vivid it was almost iridescent as oil on water, containing all colours: gold and blue and purple and green, green, green. It was beautiful, and dangerous to all those who didn't know it, its paths and its bogs, its stories and its rules.

Nara stopped crunching the beetle and swooped to land near Ysolda's head, kneading her hair like a large, feathered cat. It was quite painful, and the juice from the beetle was seeping into her plait, but Ysolda knew Nara was trying to say sorry, in her own sea hawk way.

'It's not your fault,' she said, reaching a finger up to Nara, who nipped it lightly. 'I wasn't close really.'

It was the truth, and it punched her in the heart. She had been so sure that today of all days, she'd get somewhere. She'd woken with a tug in her toes, a tingle like her feet knew where to go. She'd lifted Hari's amulet from where it hung by the door, and her feet had led her to this spot in the forest, an invisible path snaking through the trees and ending at this clearing beneath the oldest tree of the wood. It was a pull, a charge as strong as lightning plucking at the matter of the sky, and it had brought her here. She was sure of it. But what for?

There were some in their village who could scent water and ore wherever they were, dowsers who could pluck a stick from the forest floor and charge it with their spirit, send it swinging and sniffing out hidden streams, or seams of shining silver and lead. Still others would never be hungry a moment in the forest, knowing as they did every type of leaf and moss, every mushroom and every insect by sight.

Most prized were the listeners like Hari, who knew trees and understood the language of their roots, the routes they took to pass messages of water or danger, or an unnatural turn in the air. It was none of it magic, only a special sort of attention, but it might well have been to Ysolda, who could not scent, nor see, nor listen. She felt a connection to her twin tree, of course, the tree planted the day of her birth and growing a ring for each year she grew, but it didn't talk to her. The forest was a vast silence, and she longed to hear it speak.

Hari found it too loud – where other villagers had built their crofts from the plentiful wood of the coastal forest, after Hari was born their parents had had to rebuild their own with stone. She couldn't have wooden buttons on her clothes, and even the amber amulet, being fossilised sap from their Elder Alder, had to be kept on a hook unless she needed to listen.

Now their parents were dead, Hari would drag a complaining Ysolda to the cliffs to roll home slabs of slick black slate on logs to repair their roof, or heat-holding sandstone for their floor. They could not even burn wood because Hari heard it screaming. They used only peat, which smoked their house out, making it smell like Clya's smokehouse with its hanging kippers and cloudy-eyed mackerel. Even with these precautions, some days Hari stopped up her ears with beeswax and sheep's wool to keep the clamour of the trees from her head.

The Elder Alder was dazzling in the late afternoon sunlight, leaves burnished and the deep grooves of the Ogham alphabet illuminated. Ysolda soothed herself by reciting them aloud – the grid of *ae*, the nest-like weave of *ar*, the diamond of *oi*. She could read them as well as Hari, though it was learned by heart rather than inscribed there. *But just because one thing is nature and another thing skill, does not make it less special.* Easy for Hari to say.

Ysolda watched the light trailing long fingers through the leaves above her, fine mist-like rain shimmering as though suspended in amber, making her squint as it hit her pale grey eyes.

Before Hari became busy with her gift, she and Ysolda would come to learn the alphabet, to tell stories of the planting of this ancient tree, of the forest that once stretched to the End-World Wood, covering the entire country. Ysolda loved telling stories, though sometimes hers were a touch too convincing. Lies, Hari called them, but Ysolda thought there was nothing wrong with a little imagination.

Still, it was a long walk home and it would be dark soon. Now the festival of Mabon was approaching, signalling the turn of the season, the sun seemed to drop out of the sky like a hawk diving rather than sinking slowly as a feather as in summer.

'Home now, Nara,' she said, pushing herself up and buckling on her shoes. She retrieved the amulet, turning it around in her hand. It was slightly too big for her palm and shaped like a stretched-out raindrop, its pointed tip crenated like an oak leaf, its surface marked with the brush-like lines of *nion*, ash, meaning, 'open': open your ears to the forest. *I'm trying*, thought Ysolda.

She needed to return it before Hari realised and besides, she was hungry. The handful of blackberries her foraging had yielded that morning was a distant memory, and Hari was making goose pie for dinner, with real butter churned herself and flavoured with parsley picked from the herb patch outside their house. Ysolda's stomach gurgled again, and she sucked her purpled fingers for a taste of the berries.

Nara took flight and lifted suddenly out of sight. Before Ysolda realised what she was planning, the hawk was plunging back through the leaves, and the sparrow was suddenly silent.

'Nara!' Ysolda shuddered and hurried to the thick bracken where Nara had disappeared. 'Not the little ones!'

Ysolda was squeamish about these things, though she tried not to be. Hari had warned her when she had decided she wanted to train a sea hawk that you could not train it out of its nature. This was another thing Hari had been right about, though in Ysolda's mind her sister's tabby cat, Sorrell, was far crueller than Nara ever was. At least the hawk did not play with her food before killing it.

Nara was hunched over her meal, broad wings hiding it from view.

'Nara, come.'

The hawk turned her imperious head towards Ysolda. A strip of grey fur was hanging from her beak, and Ysolda's empty tummy churned.

'Nara, come. Home.'

Nara swallowed, and lowered her beak for more. Ysolda reached for her impatiently, and then froze. Sparrows did not have fur, grey or otherwise. She knew Nara had probably just caught a squirrel, but something did not feel right.

Her hawk was in a place clear of bracken and fern, lit with the last sunlight, a circle that echoed in miniature where Ysolda had sat waiting for the trees to speak to her. But it was mossy beneath the remains of Nara's kill, and moss grew only in shadow.

Ysolda's mind worked, but it was too slow. Even as she gasped her hawk's name and went to pull her clear, something tightened around Nara's feet. The bird felt the shift in the ground, her wide wings stretching to lift her away, but it was too late.

'Nara!'

The snare tightened, and like a pebble loosed from a slingshot, Nara was yanked away. Ysolda ran after her, the thin soles of her rabbit-skin shoes yielding to the brambles as she fumbled through them, thorns tearing her clothes. The hawk's cries were just in front of her, just out of sight, but Ysolda kept up, legs aching, heart hammering, eyes fixed ahead.

So focused was she on reaching her hawk that she did not notice the change in the light, the sudden thickening dark, the ground becoming boggy underfoot. If she had stopped to look down, there would have been a root or line of stones engraved with X, Ogham for *danger*. But it was not until the arm reached out and caught her about the waist that she realised she was in a trap, too.

CHAPTER TWO

OG

Since childhood, Ysolda had been told what to do if she ever found herself stuck in a bog – not that a Glaw Wood dweller should ever be so foolish as to step in one. *Still your body, spread your weight, swim.* But now, as she found her ankles sinking, her feet stuck in cold, sucking mud, a stranger's strong arm clamped around her, all the calming words vanished from her head. She screamed, and struggled, and would have lost her balance had the arm not been gripping her so tightly.

'Stop!' the voice commanded, hoarse and loud.

'Let me go!' Ysolda scratched at the arm and tried to bite it, but it was clad in coarsely woven wool that tasted worse than it smelled. She spat and retched. She could hear Nara screeching, hear the cracking air beneath her wings, but she couldn't see the hawk, couldn't see who held her.

'You need to stop,' said the voice – a boy's, she thought. The arm was thin but vice-like, the hand bunched in her clothing grimy with muck.

'Let go!'

'If I let go, you'll fall. If you fall, you'll sink. You need to stop struggling.'

Despite her fear and fury, Ysolda knew the stranger was right. Already the mud was inching up her calves, and with every twist the ground strengthened its grip. She stilled, gasping as panic squeezed her heart tighter and tighter, a fist closing about a desperate bird.

'Good. Now I'm going to let go, and pass you this stick.'

The stranger released her and Ysolda swayed, nearly falling, but she clenched her stomach and managed to stay upright. A long, plank-like branch entered her periphery, inched out over the boggy ground like a raft. It took all her will not to lunge for it; she had to move slowly. Nara was still screeching, still out of sight, and though Ysolda was almost certain this person did not want her dead, she could not be sure they didn't mean her or her hawk harm.

Lowering herself carefully as the bog moved closer to her knees, she kneeled on the plank. She had to twist painfully, her ankles still held down as though tied, and as she lay on her belly along the length of the wood, she felt the muscles straining, every one of her bones clicking in protest.

'Pull yourself forward.'

'My ankles—'

'The worst that happens is they break.' The voice was completely unconcerned.

'Oh, is that all?' snapped Ysolda. She could see their hands holding the wood steady, the knuckles showing like acorns with the effort. They were large hands, dark skinned and long fingered – splayed against the wood, they reminded Ysolda of a spider.

'This branch will sink soon.' The stranger sounded bored now, the grip on the plank loosening, and Ysolda scowled, unable to keep the bite from her voice despite her fear.

'Broken ankles it is, then.'

Taking a firm hold of the plank, mud scraping its way under her nails, she heaved herself along the rough wood. Her ankles wrenched, her shoes were torn from her feet, but though the bones popped and ached, they did not break. With a sudden squelching sigh, the bog released her, and Ysolda scrabbled her way along the plank, the stranger moving clear as she tumbled on to the firm, mossy ground.

Any stranger to Glaw Wood couldn't have been blamed for not seeing the bog. It blended perfectly with the uneven ground. The green sludge lay innocent once more, aside from where she had churned it up. But there, as she'd guessed there would be, was a root jutting from the ground with its carved X. Even without this, she could have smelled it, should have seen the subtle blur where liquid met land.

The plank of wood was already being swallowed. Queasiness rocked Ysolda's stomach as she watched the bubbles of air displaced by the sinking branch. Panting hard, she squinted up into a brown face, dark as she was pale, eyes deep, golden brown and large as Hari's. A girl, with a strong, determined chin and a low brow, hair cropped short and so dirty it could have been any colour.

Her lip was pulled back in a smirk, showing surprisingly white teeth, and Ysolda rolled herself angrily on to her side and pushed herself upright. Her soles cringed on the cold moss and her ankles felt bruised, but she was careful to keep any sign of pain from her face. Her hawk's cries were still loud as ever, but she couldn't see her anywhere in the dense foliage that crowded to the edge of the deadly clearing.

'Where's Nara?' she snarled. She was taller than the other girl, and now she stepped up close to her, hoping to seem looming and scary, though she felt like she might faint.

'Who?'

'My sea hawk.'

'Is that what it is.'

'She's not *it*, she's *she*.'

A flutter caught her eye, and with an icy jab of fury she saw Nara bundled in a fine string net hung from a nearby tree, her beautiful wings caught at odd angles as she fought to free herself.

Ysolda shouldered past, already reaching for her knife, but as she brushed against the stranger's stinking cloak, a bright flash of metal caught her eye. A moment later the girl had a weapon in her hand, so bright and gleaming it could have been newly forged. Ysolda's knife looked like a toy beside it.

'Don't touch my dinner.'

'Dinner?' The word came out like a yelp.

'Don't have good manners, do you? You've not even thanked me for helping you out of the bog.'

The smirk hadn't left her face, and Ysolda resisted the urge to punch her, eyeing the weapon. It was a spear, no simple throwing stick, forged from moon-bright metal and engraved with ornate runnels that would channel blood away from the tip so as to keep the holder's grip certain even in the heat and chaos of battle. It was a warrior's spear, too fine and too large for this slight and filthy girl. She must have stolen it, just like she was trying to steal Nara.

'It's your fault I was in there. You took Nara, and now I'm getting her back.' More bravely than she felt, Ysolda turned her back on the glinting blade and started towards her hawk, but a moment later her legs were swiped from under her by the spear's haft.

She fell forward, hard, jarring her wrists as the girl tutted. 'If you're going to do something, just do it. Don't tell people the plan if you don't want it ruined.'

Humiliated as well as furious, Ysolda kicked out, sending the girl tumbling. She snatched at the girl's wrist, managing to wrest the spear free and clumsily turned it on her attacker.

'Like that?'

The girl gave a delighted shout of surprise, but it turned into a grunt as Ysolda elbowed her hard in the stomach, levered herself up and ran to Nara, taking great care not to nick her wings as she sliced through the net. The hawk tumbled free and gathered her great wings beneath her, flapping hard to catch herself before she hit the ground. She gave an indignant cry and settled high in the tree she had been hung from, the thin snare still dangling from her talons.

Now her hawk was free and at a safe height, Ysolda rounded on the girl, who was sitting up on her elbow massaging her stomach where she'd been winded. Ysolda was furious to see she had not managed to wipe the smirk from her face.

She was a strange sight, with her black hair worn in the short style of a boy, one longer part left to grow behind her right ear, braided and stoppered with a green glass bead. Her cloak seemed to be of loom-spun wool, dyed the deep red of winterberries. This again contrasted with her tunic, which was more patch than cloth, and reeking.

The impression was of someone who had grabbed every element of themselves from elsewhere, a rich man and a poor boy, a fastidious noblewoman and a beggar, and cobbled it together to create something new. No doubt this was exactly how she had come across all her garments: she was a thief through and through.

'Now what?' said the girl.

'What do you mean "now what"?' snapped Ysolda.

'Normally the one with the spear makes the decisions.' She pushed herself upright, slapping her filthy palms together. 'If you give it back, I'll be happy to take over.'

'Stay there,' Ysolda commanded, trying to keep the tremble from both her voice and her wrist – the spear was very heavy. 'Don't move.'

The girl manoeuvred herself languidly, crossing her legs and tilting her head. Her eyes were a confusing shade of goldish brown, like wild honey. 'Or what?'

Ysolda's grip on the spear slipped and it dropped to the mossy ground, the blade so sharp it sliced deep. The girl hooted with laughter as Ysolda tugged on it, but it was jammed. She hissed in frustration, took two stomping steps and jabbed her finger at the girl. 'Just leave us alone!'

Whistling for Nara to follow, she turned her back on the still-laughing stranger and ran barefoot for home.

CHAPTER THREE

RIFT

Place names were not much use in Glaw Wood. Every person, every family, every village had a different name for the same things, and the landmarks, so far as they went, were trees or else low stone bridges that were often little more than rocks sunk into the riverbed. Even Ogham was used for generalities: *water, danger, crossing.*

So if you wanted to find your way to the sea, you might be told to take the turn by the Elder Alder, or the twist by the First Trunk, both names for the same ancient tree that marked the easiest road. Looking for the path north, you could be offered a route across the Step Stones, or else the Bright Bont, and find they were the same bridge. But there was one place everyone knew by its one name.

The Rhyg might have been called a valley were it gentle,

but 'rift' was really the only word for it. No river had carved its way through the black slate and shining quartz, and the mountains had not risen slowly through eras, rolling the forest on its back like a gentle wave. It had been created in a handful of violent moments when the landscape had torn suddenly, within living memory of Glaw Wood's oldest inhabitants.

They would tell you it was like a mighty seam splitting, a rocky root cracking, that it shook the birds from the trees like rain and sent them screaming into the sky. That it was the most unnatural thing to ever happen here. Where once there was a village atop a hill, now the tumbled ruins of homes lay scattered along a jagged rip in the earth, and deeper still had fallen people and livestock that not even the longest ropes could reach.

The forest was quick to recover and reclaim the ragged teeth that lined the jaw of the Rhyg, furring it with ferns and fungus, but the people were more reluctant. It was a graveyard of sorts, and there were stories of hauntings, of the fallen dead rising on moonless nights and calling for their lost children, rattling ghostly pots and pans as they searched for their long-buried hearths.

Apart from that, the air in this place did not feel right. It was cooler for one thing, even on the rare summer days, and in winter the frost snapped over the rift like a trap. It made the slate slopes slippery as glass, and treacherous icicles grew in sharp needles from the trees.

But still, return people did. For all its calamity, the Rhyg had been the site of Glaw Wood's largest settlement for good reason, and those reasons had only increased since the ground split itself in two. It was far enough from the wolf queen's territories to the east and the rebel lord's land to the north, and within smelling distance of the sea to the west – only a steep scramble down to the gently curving bay where traders would land bringing spices and stories.

At its tip was the intersection of two springs that fast resolved into rivers, one of them claiming the rift as its new path. The cold air was sweet and held enough rain to grow the place greener than any other, but cool enough to keep crops from rot. Its links to the fabled End-World Wood were deep and cherished, the Elder Alder being the last tree of that once-mighty forest to exist this far south. It was a good place to live, and the story of its terrifying creation kept enough people away to allow those who returned to keep large and sprawling compounds that blurred into one another's bounds.

Like everything in Glaw Wood, Ysolda's village had any number of names. Before the rift, it was mostly known as *Bryn Uchel*, the High Hill, but now the traders and hunters who passed through asked if they had reached the Sunken Settlement, or else the Broken Peak. But Ysolda simply called it home.

As she approached its sharp slant, Nara flying high above, she felt the familiar sense of calm it always placed over her, as though its shadows were a cosy blanket wrapping about her shoulders. The green smell of the thickening trees, the sound of the river, so far down it was out of sight, soothed her furious heart, and unclenched her jaw.

Who *was* that creature, with her snares and stolen spear, her filthy face and white teeth? Ysolda had never seen teeth so clean. Despite Hari's best efforts with spearmint and salt paste, their own were strong but yellowed and jumbled as a miskept drystone wall. She ran her tongue across their uneven ridges, her jarring ankles and muddy trousers a reminder of the bog's sucking hold. Nara's shadow swooped overhead and Ysolda shuddered at the memory of her cries, her wings caught in the net. *Dinner.* How could someone say such a thing? She was a beast, and she was cruel, and she was a thief. With very nice teeth.

Ysolda's bare feet gripped the cold stone – she would have to tell Hari about the girl, of course. Aside from her missing shoes and muddy clothes, she needed to explain why she was returning so late. She gripped the amulet in her pocket, and hoped her sister would not be too annoyed she'd borrowed it without asking. It was a cherished object, the source of many stories, but Hari always said it was as much Ysolda's as hers. The goose pie would be cooking in the fire, her favourite fur blanket placed within warming distance of the flames. Hari would heat water for her using fire stones placed in the tin bath, and would brush Ysolda's hair with her soft fingers and sing tales of the forest. However wrong the day had gone, Hari would make it right.

Wind gripped the trees overhead, shaking rain from their leaves to land cold and heavy as pebbles on Ysolda's head. She drew her cloak closer around herself. The wind was always fierce, funnelled as it was down the rift's seam, but the trees usually offered more protection, breaking the icy front into smaller snakes that weaved around the trunks.

This wind, though, was bitter, biting her ears. Above her, Nara shrieked her disapproval as the current was snatched from under her wings. She dived down and landed heavily on Ysolda's waiting forearm, and Ysolda drew her cloak about the bird, who, for a sea hawk, was remarkably averse to cold weather and discomfort. With the hawk fussing and nuzzling against her, Ysolda bent her head against the wind and walked on.

The first houses of their settlement started to appear through the trees, constructed of moss and wood so you might have walked right past them if you did not know they were there. Gwyn and Gwen's stood at the midpoint of the Rhyg, which meant Ysolda was halfway home. Sometimes the couple would wait for her and give her warmed milk from their sour ewes sweetened with purple-heather honey. They'd never had children, and as the youngest in the settlement, Ysolda was much doted on. But though she would have welcomed a cup of their kindness now, the door was fastened shut and the windows stoppered up with fleece forced between the wooden slats.

Ysolda frowned, the wind making her eyes water. She was not so late returning. Their shutters were usually wide open, the smell of stew filling the air. She pushed on, the wind growing stronger at her back, helping her up the hill and stuffing her ears with its needling whistles.

'Stop that,' she hissed at Nara, who was sharpening her beak against the shoulder bark, occasionally stabbing Ysolda's skin with the tip. The sound of beak against stone set her teeth on edge.

She passed more houses, each standing quiet and shuttered. As she reached the last crossing before their house, a door swung open a crack, and Fyona's thin face peered out at her. Her lips were moving, but the wind was too loud for Ysolda to hear. Fyona gestured her over.

'Inside,' she hissed, clasping Ysolda's hand with icy fingers. 'Quick.'

Before Ysolda could open her mouth, the woman had pulled her into the dark interior of her house. Living as they did with skies often clouded with rain, the inhabitants of Glaw Wood were masters of light. They built their houses with clever vents and slats to let the smoke out and the sparse sun in. Usually Fyona's house was filled with greenish light, but all the slats were stuffed with fleece and moss, just like Gwyn and Gwen's. Even the fire was out, an unheard of thing in any house in these parts, so when Fyona closed the door they were plunged into a black so complete they might have been underground. It was this that moved Ysolda to speech, though she didn't get far. 'What—'

'Shhh!' Fyona groped for her arm again and led her through the small room with a large table at its centre and an immense fireplace around which the family could sleep in winter. She pulled Ysolda to a gap behind the fireplace, Nara chittering angrily as Ysolda tripped on the hearth, and drew aside a thick woollen curtain that smelled like a pony blanket.

Behind this were the suddenly illuminated faces of Fyona's husband and children, all squatting in a tiny alcove around a caged candle. Each face was thin as Fyona's, and each was afraid. Ysolda felt another, greater stirring of unease as Fyona shoved Ysolda between her two boys and forced herself in beside her, drawing the blanket behind so they were blocked again from sight.

'What's happening?' Ysolda breathed, her knees pressed up to her chest. Nara wriggled free, digging her talons into Ysolda's tunic in order to pull herself up on to her shoulder. Beside her, Fyona's eldest, Alec, found himself eye to eye with a rumpled and disgruntled hawk, and turned quickly away.

'Quick,' said Fyona shortly. She was looking up, at something affixed to the back of the flue that took smoke out of the house. Ysolda followed her gaze and realised how Fyona had known she was passing.

There was a highly polished square of tin attached to the flue, angled so it reflected the view of yet another piece of tin that protruded out of the roof high above them. It showed the portion of wood outside Fyona's front door, the reflection only a little distorted by the natural warp in the tin's surface.

Ysolda peered at it, seeing nothing out of the ordinary: the leafy green of an oak tree, whipped by the crazed wind; in the distance, the dark stone that marked the steep drop of the Rhyg. Then the flash of a red cloak, stark as a warning against the green.

Alec was trembling. He was a strong boy, tall and broad as his mother.

'From the Lakes,' he whispered. Now Ysolda understood why he trembled. 'Ryders.'

CHAPTER FOUR

RYDERS

'Look,' Alec said, but they had all seen. On the far edge of the Rhyg came definite movement. Not the swaying of trees or the swooping of birds – horses, and on their backs Ryders in crimson cloaks, the kind every child of Glaw Wood had heard about in stories, dreamed of in nightmares.

Ryders from across the border, where the wolf queen ruled. The wolf queen who had conquered eight of the world's twelve realms before coming to the Isles: whole king- and queendoms falling to her rule, countries vaster than Ysolda had imagination for. Until today, Ryders in Glaw Wood were but a child's tale. But this was no fable, and though Ysolda pinched her arm, she did not wake up.

'Hari,' she breathed. 'Does Hari know?'

'The trees will surely tell her?' said Fyona, her eyes not moving from the tin.

But some bone-deep thing told Ysolda that Hari could not hear them. Hari's ears were stopped up with wax, their stone house silent. Her amulet, the fossilised sap tapped from the Elder Alder that could warn her, sat dumb in Ysolda's pocket.

Ysolda's heart began to knock against her ribs. The trees would find a way to tell her. This girl who listened and guarded them and their secrets both, always. They would strain their roots and knock aside the unfeeling stone, force their splinters from the hinges and scream for her—

The Ryders' red cloaks were shocking against the gentle hues of the forest. They carried spears strapped to their backs, and Ysolda recognised the weapons as the same as the girl's. They rode their horses right to the edge of the Rhyg.

'They can't jump that,' said Fyona. She was rocking slightly, sending Alec's knee into Ysolda's. 'They'll have to go around. It'll take hours.'

Fyona's husband murmured his agreement, his arm tight around their younger son, Merfyn. The Ryders' cloaks became a murky brown as they turned their backs and walked their horses back into the shadowed forest. Alec let out a long, whistling breath. Ysolda felt every muscle of his body relax. Her own heart started to slow and she readied herself to uncoil, to hurry home and warn Hari. They had time.

But then, movement again – a blur of red as the Ryders broke free of the trees. Ysolda heard the pounding hooves, the whinnying cries of the horses louder even than the wind—

'They won't clear the rift!' Alec gasped, and Fyona's husband pulled Merfyn's head into his side so he would not see.

The Ryders stood out of their saddles and led their horses in the impossible jump. Midway across the rift they seemed to hover, suspended as Nara in flight, and then one, two, three landed hard before Fyona's house. A fourth disappeared into the gaping maw of the Rhyg, but the fifth, knowing he would fall short, threw himself forward from his horse and landed on his forearms, dragging himself up the slick rocks to safety.

'The horses,' cried Ysolda, horrified, and Fyona reached across her son and clamped her cold hand across Ysolda's mouth.

'I know, I know, I know,' she whispered soothingly. 'Don't look. Don't speak.'

But Ysolda couldn't look away. She felt sick that the Ryders would risk themselves like that, risk their horses. What had brought them here that they needed so urgently? Nara's talons dug into her shoulder, and a moment later the hawk took off up the flue, forcing her way on to the mossy roof and sending fragments scattering down over them.

'Nara,' hissed Ysolda. She tried to whistle for the hawk, but Nara was perched atop the roof, her feathery flank blocking the tin mirrors.

'Nara!' dared Ysolda, a little louder, and the hawk shifted, allowing them a partial view of the Ryders. They had pulled the unseated rider on to the back of another horse and seemed not to have noticed Fyona's house, or else had no interest in it. Again, Ysolda felt Alec's body loosen as they turned the horses to travel down the slope.

Ysolda felt like she might cry with relief. They were moving away from her house, out of the valley. Towards the sea. She turned to Fyona, a strained smile on her face, but the woman was staring back, her eyes wide and wild in the candlelight.

'Ysolda,' she said. 'You have to stay.'

'What?'

'Hari will be all right.'

'I know,' said Ysolda, frowning.

But as Nara once more smothered the mirror, and let out a warning cry, realisation gripped Ysolda tight as talons. The tin square showed her a mirror image. The Ryders were not travelling down, but up. Towards the sisters' stone house.

As the red cloaks vanished from sight, Ysolda scrambled from her place. She threw aside the blanket, knocking the candle to the floor, where it extinguished with a hiss of smoke. Plunged once more into blackness, Ysolda felt for the door.

'Ysolda!'

Ignoring Fyona's warning shout, she blundered on, knocking into the table. Her thigh stung, and behind her, she heard Fyona curse as she knocked over a chair in pursuit. She heard Alec calling his mother, and as Ysolda flung open the door, she looked back and saw Fyona being wrestled to safety by her sons and husband.

She threw the door closed and whistled for Nara, who soared overhead as Ysolda began to run, pure terror burning in her chest, for home.

The wind was still with her, speeding her pace, but it was at the Ryders' backs too, and they had horses. They must be heading for her house. There were no other homes this way, and beyond it was the plunge of the Rhyg, a dead end. In her pocket the amulet tumbled, heavy with betrayal. How could she have taken it, Hari's one link to the forest? Above her, Nara screeched, and Ysolda longed to be able to see what she saw, to know what lay ahead.

She broke free of the treeline, reaching the world of rock they had made their home. Her lungs were tight as a noose as she heaved herself over a bluff, cutting out the easier switchbacks for the fastest route. As she wedged her foot tightly into a crevice, reaching out to lever herself up, the wind dropped. Without it to press her flat to the rock face, she lost her balance, gripping on to a knot of tree root to keep herself from falling. She clutched tight, panting hard.

The sudden silence was eerie, like being plunged underwater, as though she was back in the bog and sunk down into the belly of the earth. And then came a feeling she had never felt before, a dread so endless she wanted to scream, and below her hands the rock seemed to pulse like a giant, cold heart.

She scuttled from the dizzying edge of the Rhyg as Nara wheeled over her, still screeching, but the screeches were distant, and beneath Ysolda the rock pulsed again, a repulsive, convulsive movement, like the ground was caught in spasm. And then it began to tremble. Sounds rushed in again, a mighty rumbling like a storm sweeping in off the sea, shaking the entire forest. Nara let out a warning cry, and Ysolda turned in time to see the Rhyg rip itself further, a crack opening in the ground and chasing towards her.

She threw herself backwards, roots and branches raining down from the bluff above her, then pebbles and rocks and slices of slate as the whole rock face began to crumble. She ran, but there was nowhere safe, nowhere to go. The trees fell below her in a great wave as the Rhyg tore, Nara screeched, and Ysolda fled as the world broke apart around her.

She crouched in a patch of clear ground, pressing herself into the earth, feeling it writhe and dance and rip, and suddenly still. She lay panting, dirt like metal in her mouth, and felt Nara land atop her back, nipping with her beak. Her ears rang, and dimly she heard hooves. She crawled for cover on shaking arms, wriggling into a hollowed-out cave newly revealed by the quake. She was not a moment too slow, for a second later the ground thudded again with horses. She raised her head in time to see the Ryders' red cloaks whip out of sight, down a freshly riven path in the Rhyg.

Up, she thought in her terror, *up*, and her exhausted and bruised body obeyed, propelling her over the ground, along the switchbacks and over the final bluff. She straightened, Nara landing heavily on her forearm, and opened her mouth to call for Hari. But her voice died in her throat.

The Rhyg had swallowed their stone home.

CHAPTER FIVE

TAKEN

Ysolda lost what strength remained in her body and fell to her knees, sending Nara once more flying into the air. The Rhyg had opened beneath the foundations and gulleted the house entire. Where once were walls, and a door, and a roof, now was nothing but a pit, about its edges rubble, still loose and tumbling into a deep chasm.

It had the sickening, sucking power of a whirlpool, and on her hands and knees Ysolda crawled to the edge, lay on her belly and looked down. There was nothing to see: it was like peering into a starless night sky. Black as tar, and endless. The air was cold, drawing into the darkness like some mighty creature drew breath, calling her towards it. Nara hovered over, flapping her wings to keep from being pulled down by the mysterious current.

'Hari?' Ysolda's voice was a whisper, lost instantly to the dark. She gripped the amulet, as though her sister could speak to her through it. Beneath her, the ground gave a weak tremble, and Ysolda could not even summon the strength to move away from the edge. If there was another quake, she would be tumbled into the depths, like their house. Like—

'Hari?'

All her tears were caught in her throat. She could not even bring herself to cry. Her heart beat loud in her ears and her head felt stuffy. It could not be. None of this was real.

The sucking of the pit felt stronger, tugging on her plait, pulling at her fingertips where they gripped the black rock that had once been the path leading to their doorway. The narrow bed they shared, the pot they cooked in, Sorrell asleep on the woven rushes . . .

Another tremor, and the rock she was holding crumbled like dust. Nara gave a second warning cry but it was far away now. It would be so easy to move a fraction forward, to let the balance of her body tip and take her down. The ground rumbled, and Ysolda breathed in the cold, sucking air. It tasted of moss and iron. The black of the pit was so complete it felt like looking into a night sky.

'Are you mad?'

The voice made her jump. The skin of her throat burned

as someone grabbed the back of her tunic and yanked her away. She felt the seams tear, Hari's careful stitches coming apart under her weight, and she reared up angrily, turning to face—

'You?'

The short-haired stranger stood before her, rock dust covering her face, speckling the bristles on her head.

'Yes, me, and don't think I'll be making a habit of saving your life.'

Ysolda sat dazed on the ground. She still felt the pull of the pit but it was fainter now, easier to resist. Her shock was wearing thinner, and she felt the edges of pain needle her chest. The stranger's cloak was the same red as the Ryders' and a hot-cold wave of sickness washed over her.

The stranger whistled. 'Some quake that was. I nearly got squashed.'

'Go away,' said Ysolda.

The stranger ignored her, striding past Ysolda, her flapping cloak revealing the stolen spear strapped to her back. Nara snipped her beak angrily as she passed, but the girl only gazed into the chasm, seeming immune to its pull. 'I'm looking for Angharad. She lives at the top of the rift. Is this it?'

Her sister's name in the stranger's mouth sent hot prickles of nausea through Ysolda's body.

'Well?' said the girl, tilting her head so the bead of her

braid clicked against the clasp of her cloak. 'Is this the Rhyg?'

'Yes,' Ysolda croaked.

'And this is the top? Well, that's obvious I suppose. So where is the stone house? Did I miss it?'

She looked back down the slope and Ysolda followed her gaze, saw how utterly her home had been changed in a matter of moments. The Rhyg had ripped itself twice as wide, felling trees, leaving roots upturned like arms raised in distress. The river was gone, flowing somewhere at its dark base, and the birds were silent, the wind still. It was eerie, and she trembled.

'Here,' she said hoarsely. She pointed at the chasm.

The stranger frowned, and then her thick eyebrows lifted. 'Oh. The quake?' She scanned the depths and sighed as though it was an inconvenience and not a catastrophe. 'And Angharad?'

'Hari,' murmured Ysolda, and now the tears broke past the dam of shock and flooded down her cheeks. 'My sister.' She wrapped her arms around her knees and sobbed. Her heart was breaking; she could feel it shattering like the rock around them, and not even Nara's weight landing on her shoulder was a comfort. She was lost, and nothing would ever be right again.

'She . . .' The stranger made no move to comfort her, but her voice became softer. 'She was home?'

Ysolda continued sobbing, Nara swaying on her shoulder as her body convulsed.

'There were Ryders,' the stranger said. 'Did they get to her before the quake?'

Ysolda's thoughts reeled and tangled. 'I . . . Maybe. Why?' She eyed the stolen spear. 'Do you know them?'

'They were here before the quake?'

'Yes.'

'Then they probably have her.'

'Hari?' Ysolda rubbed the tears from her cheeks. 'They were here for her?'

The girl nodded impatiently. 'I would have beaten them to it if not for our little interlude at the bog.'

'So she's . . . she's not . . .'

They both looked down into the ripped rocks. The girl shrugged with sickening nonchalance. 'If they found her, they'll have taken her.'

Ysolda stumbled to her feet, ears ringing. 'I have to go after them. Do you know where they were going? Why did they take her?'

The girl crossed her arms. 'Are you a listener too?'

'Why?'

'Because if you are, you need to stay as far away from the Ryders as possible. They're looking for anyone gifted – listeners, diviners, dowsers, even healers.'

'I'm none of those,' said Ysolda. 'I'm nothing.'

'That's the spirit,' said the girl.

'But why are they taking them?'

'For her, of course.'

There was no need for the girl to elaborate. The slight tremor in her voice was enough. Her. She. The wolf queen, Seren. Ruler of the Lakes, speaker of wolves. Many names, none of them gentle, none of them kindly. Her realms had once grown steadily and violently every year, her armies bolstered by sea wolves that patrolled the borders.

But she had settled here, in the Isles, twenty years ago and claimed only the central belt of the Lakes for herself. Not the fertile, rolling hills of the Suthridge, nor the eeling grounds of the Fens. She had not attempted a capture of Thane Boreal's northern lands with its forests full of blue-painted Kalti warriors. Just the high mountains and wild coast and wide calm pools of the Lakes. There she staked her territory, sea wolves at every border, troubling her neighbours only in the leanest years. She herself rode a wolf, and was said to have teeth sharp as knives, eat raw meat, see in the dark—

'What's she going to do with her?' Ysolda's voice was a rasp.

'She's looking for something, for someone. She's taking anyone who might help her find them.'

'Hari can't help.'

'She speaks with trees,' said the girl, eyebrow raised as

she gestured around them. 'Useful if the missing person is in a forest.'

'It's my fault she didn't hear them coming,' Ysolda whispered. She held the amber out on her trembling palm. 'I took her amulet.'

A rustling sound came from a tangle of mossy birch branches. The girl swung around, pulling the heavy spear from her back.

'Wait!' Ysolda crawled forward. 'Sorrell?'

A mournful mew came from the centre of the makeshift den. Tears sprang up again in Ysolda's eyes as she reached into the heart of the branches and pulled out the terrified tabby. Sorrell quaked in Ysolda's arms, and she pressed her tight to her chest, both their pulses racing. 'I have to get Hari back,' said Ysolda. 'She has to come home.'

'It's a long way to the Lakes. And why would Seren listen to you? You've obviously heard about her – she's not the most friendly.'

'You know her?'

'I'm from the Lakes. My father was a Ryder, so I heard the plan. I came to warn your sister.'

Ysolda narrowed her eyes, holding tighter to Sorrell. 'Why?'

'Because I'm nice,' said the girl, grinning unconvincingly with all of her straight, white teeth. 'And to be honest, I don't like what she's doing. Taking people from their homes, stealing them away. But she's always one step ahead. Or several miles.' She kicked a loose stone into the Rhyg, its final echo a long time coming.

Like her clothing, nothing the girl said added up. But Ysolda clung to every word, because they meant Hari was alive. Alive, and in the wolf queen's clutches.

CHAPTER SIX

MAP

'I'm wasting time,' Ysolda said. 'I need to go after them.'

Dazedly, she dropped Sorrell to the ground and started back down the edge of the Rhyg, but again the girl caught hold of her wrist. 'That's south.' With her free hand she pointed. 'The Lakes are east.'

The impossibility of the situation washed over Ysolda like a cold faint. How was she going to do this? She had no horse, no shoes, no clothes other than what she was wearing. Nothing at all, except the blade on her belt, Nara at her shoulder, Hari's stolen amulet, Hari's cat at her feet. She clenched her eyes shut.

'Look,' said the girl, in a soft voice that made Ysolda instantly suspicious. 'You'll never catch them. But we could get ahead of them. Get to what she really wants, use it to get your sister back.'

Nara snapped her beak and Ysolda reached up to smooth the bird's ruffled feathers, chewing the inside of her cheek. *Don't worry*, she told her hawk, herself. *I'll not be taken in.*

Satisfied she had Ysolda's attention, the girl used the point of her still-drawn spear to scuff aside fallen leaves and mark out a rough shape in the ground. 'We're here.' She marked a spot with a circle. 'The Lakes are here.'

She drew border lines from one edge to another, and Ysolda realised it was a map of the Isles. She had never seen one before – the only maps she knew were the ones formed in her mind by Glaw Wood's landmarks and stories. Their nub of land, extending out into the Western Sea like a determined chin, looked very small suddenly, though Ysolda had never much cared what lay beyond it. It was enough of a world for her.

'She's searched south, east, now west, collecting gifted people wherever she goes. Now she's heading north. Here.' She drew an X in the centre of the northlands.

'That's Thane Boreal's land.'

'She's desperate,' said the girl. 'She's looking for the End-World Wood.'

Ysolda blinked dumbly, shocked at the mention of the wood in this stranger's mouth.

'Haven't you heard of it?'

'Of course I have,' snapped Ysolda. *But how have you?*

'Well then, you understand.'

Ysolda didn't, but she wasn't about to let this smug girl know that. 'Then why is she going there?' she asked, pointing at the X.

'What?'

'It's the End-World Wood,' said Ysolda, relishing knowing something the girl didn't. 'It's at the edge of the Isles. There.' She pointed to the extreme north-east of the shape, past even Thane Boreal's domain. Every Glaw Wood dweller knew the story of the wood planted on a tidal island, the roots of all its trees intertwined and vast as a cavern.

The girl considered the map, then squinted at Ysolda. 'You're sure?'

'Clue's in the name,' said Ysolda. 'Our Elder Alder is seeded from the same forest. They're sister trees.'

'Well,' said the girl, sounding faintly impressed. 'That puts us one step ahead of her.'

'You,' said Ysolda. 'I'm not involved in whatever this –' she gestured at the map – 'is.'

The girl ignored her. 'And you know who's there? Living in the central tree?'

'The Anchorite,' said Ysolda, again shocked the girl knew these things she'd presumed were Glaw Wood tales. 'But she's just a story.'

The girl shook her head, almost pityingly. 'Not true. She's become a story, but she's as real as you or me.'

At that moment, Ysolda didn't feel real. Her fingers and toes tingled with shock. Her house was gone, her sister was missing, and she was speaking to a stranger using the spear of a Ryder to draw beyond the limits of anything Ysolda had ever imagined.

'Not possible,' she said. 'No one lives that long.'

'Trees do.'

'People aren't trees.'

The girl looked at her squarely. 'The Anchorite exists. And the wolf queen knows it too. That's who she really wants. From her, everything else follows.'

'Everything else?'

The girl fixed her with a cunning gaze. 'Her ultimate goal.'

Ysolda's impatience was rising. 'Which is?'

'None of your concern. But if we can get to the Anchorite first, the wolf queen will give your sister back in return.'

'If the Anchorite exists—'

'She does—'

'And it's who she really wants—'

'It is—'

'Then why hasn't she gone there straight away?' Ysolda scuffed the cross of the End-World Wood with her boot.

'Even if she thinks it's in the wrong place, why take my sister?'

The girl stared evenly at her and shrugged.

Anger bloomed in Ysolda's chest. 'I don't believe a word you're saying. Not that the Anchorite is real, not that your father was a Ryder, none of it.'

'Not even that your sister is alive?' challenged the girl.

Ysolda scooped Sorrell up from the ground, the cat's warm, well-fed weight anchoring her. 'Come, Nara.'

The sea hawk took off from her perch, cuffing the girl around the cheek. She hissed and waved the spear at Nara's retreating tail. 'You'll regret not coming with me! You're making a mistake. And you're *still* going the wrong way.'

But Ysolda kept walking, feet jarring at every step, hers and Sorrell's hearts thumping against each other. When she reached the turn to Fyona's house, she looked back. The girl was gone, but more than that, the view was so altered it felt like a nightmare. Only a rip in the world was left in place of their stone house, the darkening grey sky huge and swallowing, seeming to press down on her.

Ysolda shivered, and hugged Sorrell closer. It would be so easy to knock on Fyona's door, crawl on to a well-stuffed mattress, lay her head on a goose-feather pillow and sink into sleep with the cat on her chest. But this wasn't a nightmare. It was real, and no matter that the girl was a thief and a liar: Ysolda knew Hari wasn't dead. She'd feel it. Her heart would have ripped, like the Rhyg. She wasn't gifted, but she was a sister.

'Ysolda?' Fyona's voice was dazed as she peered out through a crack in the door. 'What happened?'

'A quake,' said Ysolda, her own voice like someone else's. 'Our house is gone.'

Fyona opened her door wider, hand over her mouth. 'Hari?'

'The Ryders took her.'

'Come inside.' Fyona reached for her, not wanting to step out from the safety of her house. 'Quickly.'

'They're gone,' she said. 'I have to go too.'

'Don't be ridiculous,' said Fyona. 'Come in at once.'

'Will you watch Sorrell? She eats everything, even bread.' Ysolda held out the cat, and Fyona took her in trembling hands, shock making her movements slow as swim-strokes.

'Come on,' said Fyona, still looking left and right for the Ryders.

But Ysolda took a step backwards. 'She likes her nose being scratched. And don't touch her belly unless she offers it to you.'

'Ysolda, come in now. You must sleep.'

'I have to go after them.'

'You're a child, Ysolda—'

'I need to borrow some shoes. Can I? I'll bring them back.'

'No!' shouted Fyona. 'No shoes, because you're not going!'

'Fine,' said Ysolda. She felt like she was in a sort of trance. 'I'll go barefoot.'

Fyona stopped her and, her face a picture of misery, bent to beside the door and picked up a pair of boots – her own, by the looks of them. Ysolda took them with mumbled thanks and stooped to buckle them. They were only a little too big, and thick soled.

'Ysolda—' The ground rumbled, and Fyona's face drained further.

'It's all right,' said Ysolda, more to herself than anyone. 'Aftershocks.'

The ground rumbled louder, shaking under Ysolda's feet. She straightened.

'Please.' Fyona looked on the verge of tears, clutching Sorrell. 'Come inside.'

Behind her, Ysolda could see Alec and Merfyn sheltering beneath their broad oak table. She couldn't hide from what was happening. The wood would take care of her. And when she reached the edge of the wood?

Nara landed heavily on her shoulder, talons sharp even through the bark of her shoulder guard.

'Take care of Sorrell for me. Tell her I'll bring Hari home.'

Nara sensed her intention, taking off again as she started

to run. She heard the heavy thump as Fyona dropped Sorrell inside, the squeak of the door's hinges as she threw the door wide to follow her, but then Merfyn gave a fearful shout, and Ysolda knew Fyona would turn back to her crying boy. She cared for Ysolda, but not more than her children. No one cared for Ysolda like Hari did, and no one cared for Hari like Ysolda did. That was why this was the only way.

CHAPTER SEVEN

TWIN TREE

Ysolda cut south-east. The Elder Alder was not so far out of the way for the easiest route to the eastern path, and it felt foolish to leave without saying goodbye to it. She approached through its self-seeded forest, imagined the trees speaking to one another through their swaying crowns and searching roots. Did they, too, feel afraid?

The ground grumbled again, throwing her against an alder. Gwyn's alder, Ysolda knew, feeling the Ogham symbol carved into the trunk. Each of the villagers had a twin tree, a seed from the Elder Alder planted the day they were born. It would grow until they died, a ring for each year of their lives, and when it was time it would become the pyre on which their bodies were burned. She held on to the trunk until the ground settled once more. It felt like stepping from a moving ship – or at least Ysolda imagined it did. She'd never had cause to go on a boat.

She thought of the map the girl had drawn with the spear. Glaw Wood barely a handspan, their location a scratch, though Ysolda had walked and walked all her life and never unravelled its extent. She hated the girl for many reasons, but most of all for that – for making her whole world seem so insignificant, a mere mark on a map. She thought of her walking alone to the End-World Wood, a forest that was once matchless in size, and now was a myth. She'd have liked to see it, under different circumstances, but it had always seemed too far away, and anyway, it lay across the land of two dangerous rulers.

Their whole village's trees ringed their Elder Alder like a guard, children around their mother tree. She walked through them, lingering a moment at Hari's tree, still standing strong, and her own. Beside them were the stumps of their parents' trees, cut the same day twelve years ago. Her missing for them was far off now, all her memories of them planted in her by Hari. Love could live mouth to mouth, though she could not recall their faces, their voices.

She traced the engraved letters of her own name, her twin tree stretching over her head. They were carved, like all the names, deep into the bark, past the sapwood to the heartwood. It was a symbol of how intimately their fates were bound: the forest and its people. Only the Elder Alder would stand long after they were all cut down, replaced by new saplings.

She reached the central trunk and crouched a moment beside it. Could it really have been barely two hours since she sat beneath it, straining to listen? The sky was true dark now, pitted with stars, and she wondered if she should have slept, at least, in the safety of Fyona's home. She could sleep here – the alder would protect her. It always felt sacred to Ysolda, where the only order was that of trees and water and weather.

Not so in the Lakes. Even the thought of the wolf queen's dwelling place sent a chill through Ysolda's body, and she pulled her cloak closer around herself, longing for her wool cape crushed in the remains of their house. In the wolf queen's dominion they believed in an ancient system, over which one person could rule, had whole beliefs based in stories about ley lines and secret webs of earth. Ysolda tried to remember everything she'd heard that was solid about that territory, that was not merely myth or superstition as the Anchorite was.

Ysolda snorted. *The Anchorite? An ancient girl, hundreds of years old, living in the roots of the End-World Wood? She must think I'm a fool, that stranger.*

But why would she lie? Some people had it in them like a sickness. Hari said Ysolda did, though it was only storytelling. The girl's spear-drawn map rose again at her through the dark. That small shape was all she knew, the lines of the Lakes so very far away. But the forest stretched all the way to the border, and Ysolda knew her wood. She could find water and food, and Nara could keep watch for Ryders. They could navigate themselves there, by sun and stars. Ysolda pulled her flask from her belt and drained it, then set it upright in a fork of the tree's boughs, leaves folded around the edges to funnel any falling rain or gathering condensation into it. It should be full by morning.

Ysolda huddled closer to the alder's trunk, pressing her ear to it, hoping to hear its murmur. Nara landed in the lowermost branches, her vision as sharp in the dark as the day, but wary.

'Am I doing the right thing?' Ysolda asked the alder. She laid her palms on its trunk, hoping her hands might be drawn irresistibly to an Ogham symbol – perhaps *yes*, perhaps *stay*.

Ysolda felt in her pocket for the amber amulet. Perhaps this was the moment, as she was poised on the edge of a perilous journey, that the alder would deign to talk to her. She felt her obsidian blade in its protective rabbit skin, but no amulet. She checked her other pocket, and came up with only rosehips.

Kneeling, Ysolda emptied her pockets, peering through the darkness at the objects laid before her. Obsidian blade, slingshot, striking flint, gut thread she had been using to play with Sorrell that morning. Flakes of bark from her shoulder plate, that Nara had chipped away and Ysolda had absent-mindedly kept. Her heart began to thud in her ears, and she upturned the calfskin pouch on her belt. More rosehips, some hawthorn leaves, a moss-wrapped shrew's skull she'd liked for its pristine whiteness, now coated in the filth of the bog. But no amber amulet.

'Roots,' she hissed, frantic now, patting down her clothes, checking and rechecking her neck, her wrists, unbuckling her borrowed boots to check even her ankles. When had she last held it? Here, earlier. Could she have lost it in the bog?

But no, there was later, wasn't there? When she'd held it in her hand by the edge of the Rhyg, held it out to show—

'That beast!'

The stranger, the girl. She'd shown it to her, and now it was gone. Ysolda had already been certain she was a thief, and now Hari's amulet was missing. That creature had taken it. Faintly, Ysolda remembered the girl helping her up, brushing against her side. In her dazed state, Ysolda hadn't noticed the lift but now it was obvious. Her jaw ached as she clenched her teeth. What a fool she was, for showing a known enemy their most precious possession.

Not possession, Hari would say. *We are only its keepers. Its caretakers. That amulet is like a key to time, holding the past in its depths. It was formed from the first trees of our forest and contains all its wisdom – all its histories, all its futures. It's like holding a piece of starlight: ancient and vital. It must never leave the forest – it is its heartbeat, its pulse.*

And Ysolda had let that stranger steal it, and if she succeeded in her mission, the amulet would be as far from the Elder Alder as Ysolda could imagine. Angry tears pricked her eyes, and she wiped them roughly away.

'What do I do?' she said aloud, but the alder was quiet as ever, and the ground had stopped its trembling. It was as though the whole world held all its enormous breath and turned its face away from her. Despite Nara chittering in the branches, Ysolda felt painfully alone.

CHAPTER EIGHT

BOUNDARY

Ysolda's stomach woke her, rumbling almost as badly as the aftershocks of the quake. She groaned, coming slowly back into her body. The sun was already lightening the sky. She had slept solidly, dreamlessly. Now it was early, and there was no time to waste. She retrieved her flask, full of crisp dew and sweet rain, stoppering it with its engraved cork.

Whistling for Nara, she waited. The hawk would be close by, feeding on some unlucky early bird. Sure enough, the branches to Ysolda's left rustled, and the sea hawk swooped low over her head, dropping a cracked-off branch of bullaces, small bitter plums that Hari loved.

'Thank you,' murmured Ysolda, holding out her arm for Nara to land. The sea hawk chattered against her cheek.

Ysolda stripped the fruits from the branch and chewed one, finding its small pit and spitting it on to the ground beneath the alder. Perhaps it would grow, perhaps it would dissolve into food for the older tree. It was a last offering, until Ysolda could return.

'Don't be so dramatic,' she told herself, packing the rest of the bullaces into her pocket, cushioning them with leaves so they wouldn't bruise. 'You'll be home before you know it.'

She started to walk. The day was brisk, the sky only lightly veiled in wispy clouds like sheep's wool. The weather changed by the hour here, but Ysolda reckoned they'd escape heavy rain for today at least. She'd walked this way before, trailing Hari who was out listening, trying to track the source of a rot that was blighting beechnuts. Each part of the forest was essential to the whole, and even small sickness must be treated quickly. This was why Hari was so prized in their village – she could not only hear, but smell the pain of the trees.

Like bitter smoke, she'd said, *like chewing raw hawthorn*. Wind was hardly in short supply in Glaw Wood, so the scents would float to her, and so long as it did not change direction too often, she could track them with incredible accuracy, like a bloodhound.

They'd walked two days, spending the night beneath a dying oak that had moaned to Hari all night. She'd woken hollow eyed and haunted, and had used Ysolda's obsidian to cut the final living roots, to speed its demise.

'Mercy is better than pity,' she'd said, and the words felt special to Ysolda, summing up all Hari was. She not only listened, she acted, even when it pained her to do so.

They'd found the source of the rot late the next afternoon, a dying beech infested with beetles. Hari sent the whole thing up in smoke, covering her ears and crying silently. Even Ysolda, who could not hear it, found herself weeping. The tree took hours to burn, lighting the night sky like a mighty candle, and they cooked beechnuts in the embers, cracking them open one by one and finding nothing but rot.

Ysolda passed the oak that sheltered them around midday. It was well on its way to full decay, even the mosses abandoning it. Ysolda remembered huddling into Hari's warm side, feeling her sister shake as the oak keened at her. Ysolda touched the mushy bark, and it flaked off in her hands.

She followed a narrow seam of black slate, along which a stream of water was running, making it slick, but she didn't want to risk softer ground, probably loosened by the quake. In all the confusion and worry of Hari's abduction, Ysolda had barely paused to think about the quake, vicious enough to shake loose her house from its foundations. Quakes were not usual here, despite the creation of the Rhyg. Before that, there had never been such a tremor. What did two within twenty years mean?

Ysolda scolded herself silently. It didn't need to mean anything at all. She was sounding like a Lakes dweller, looking for messages in nature's actions.

The channel cut deeper through a gorge Ysolda knew led to a spring, the banks rising mossy, bittercress trailing from roots. The quake had dislodged chunks of earth from the sides, so it was as though she was burrowing mole-like into the ground, the underworld of the forest laid bare in cross-section. She could see the panic of ants dislodged from their nests in the clods of mud, was careful to step over them. The roots of a hawthorn looped out like a noose, the fine tendrils of white fungi that linked them each to each – the weavings, as Hari called them – seeming soft as fur. Ysolda wondered what they were saying to one another, what messages they were carrying.

Nara was enjoying herself, Ysolda could tell. She would vanish for hours at a time, hunting in these less-familiar grounds, reaping the mice shaken from their nooks, the trout worried from calm waters into bouldered rapids. She checked in on Ysolda every now and again, bringing small gifts: half a fish – Nara had already eaten the head and guts – more bullaces, a stick of willow. Ysolda filled her pockets and her belly, grateful as ever for the hawk's company and intelligence, her seeming true care for her, though Hari often told her not to sentimentalise a wild animal.

'But you are not wild, are you, Nara?' murmured Ysolda, and Nara perched upon her shoulder for a rest. 'No more than me. We are each other's, you and I.'

The ground rose up out of the slate channel, and Ysolda refilled her flask at the spring, the water misty with chalk. She was grateful it was still daylight. When she and Hari had come this way, they'd come to the stricken beech early in the afternoon, but it was already growing cold and dark.

Ysolda arrived at bright dusk, the ash of the burnt tree long dispersed. All around it, the trees had grown their crowns to fill the gaps, drinking up the dead beech's portion of sunlight. Everything had a cycle; nothing was wasted.

As she paused, she realised she had reached it: the boundary. Her own personal crossing place, from the Glaw Wood that was known to her, to the Glaw Wood that was not. The blurred, unknown space that would gradually fade and become the Lakes.

She must not be afraid. She must think of Hari – perhaps already in the court of the wolf queen, a castle built of shipwrecks. What would the dead wood sing to her? What horrors had they seen? Ysolda shook her head, said 'No' aloud. Maybe she should not think on Hari, either.

Breathing deeply, she stepped on through the trees.

Nothing much changed. They were the same kinds of trunks she knew from home, perhaps even grown from the same mother trees and dispersed by birds or boars. But unease grew in her stomach. She was only a day's walk from home, but it was further than she'd ever gone before, further than anyone she knew had gone, apart from Gwen, who was born in the eeling fens. All the stories Ysolda had were from traders who came to Glaw Wood's western coast. This stretch had no tales she knew.

Even Nara seemed more subdued, not leaving Ysolda's shoulder, kneading the bark pad so it cracked and flaked, crackling in her ears. The path was more established, which set Ysolda's teeth on edge. The thought of people breaking this ground, people she did not know and had never seen – it felt like walking in the footsteps of ghosts.

The ground stopped its gentle rise, plateauing as a small escarpment, a single rowan in full berry bent almost double by its exposure to wind, its roots twined into a grey boulder. Suddenly the forest was laid out before her like a carpet, and Ysolda turned to see where she had walked, the paths inscrutable beneath a thick canopy of green. On a clear day, she would be able to see the sea, but of course there was no such thing in Glaw Wood. The sun was low in its curve, illuminating the clouds in dramatic shades of orange and scarlet.

She squinted ahead, in the direction of the Lakes.

Were those mountains in the distance, the peaks that protected the wolf queen's territories alongside the Ryders and wolves? Ysolda scanned the downhill slope, trying to divine the route she could take, but great boughs of rowan blocked her view. All of them were red as the clouds with berries, and Ysolda frowned. By now they should have been picked clean by blackbirds and mistle thrushes, redstarts and waxwings.

Ysolda turned a full circle, Nara swaying on her shoulder. Now she thought about it, she had not heard a bird since leaving the spot of the burnt beech. She'd thought it was because of Nara hunting, but the hawk hadn't left her shoulder since she'd crossed that imagined boundary, and seemed quiet, jumpy.

Ysolda strained to listen to the forest, but it was as though it was holding its breath, even the wind stilling a moment. A chill spread through her, but she knew not to rue her luck. The rowan berries would make a good meal, and below the boulder was a hollow, probably carved by weather as much as people. Ysolda nooked herself into the gap made soft by moss and found it mercifully dry as she crawled further in.

Nara, who hated being closed in, took off and tucked herself into the rowan above them. The berries stained Ysolda's mouth and hands as the sunset dyed the world red.

CHAPTER NINE

SMOKE

Nara's warning shriek woke her. Ysolda tried to sit up and banged her head on unforgiving rock. The moss had seeped water into her sleeve, and her arm was freezing cold. It was pitch black, but as she orientated herself, she saw a sliver of night sky ahead. She crawled carefully towards it, staying low and keeping her movements as quiet as possible. Nara called again, but the hawk did not swoop to block her exit, so Ysolda judged it safe to emerge.

Crouching, she shifted around the boulder, back pressed to the rock, scanning the surrounds. Judging by the high moon, it was the heart of night, the time it was scariest to wake.

It was not hard to see what had alarmed Nara. A column of smoke rose from the bowl of the valley ahead, perhaps only a mile off. Ysolda's heart quickened. She knew it could easily be a village, or a lone traveller, perhaps a friendly family. But the quality of the smoke worried her. It was black, suggesting young, green wood full of sap. No forest dweller would choose this type to burn. It suggested strangers.

The hawk landed heavily on her shoulder.

'What do you think, Nara?' whispered Ysolda. She was not, by nature, brave. She did not charge into hunts hollering like Fyona's son Alec, and felt faint at the sight of blood. Everything in her body wanted to root her to the spot, turn her face from the smoke and go back to sleep in her safe hole of rock and moss. But those types of decisions were far away now. If that fire meant Ryders, perhaps it meant Hari.

Mouth dry, Ysolda descended the slope, grateful for the mossy ground and trees in full leaf muffling her steps. Over her head, the red rowan berries glimmered silver in the moonlight. Before too long she could smell the fire, nosing towards it, and then voices. Men and women, grown-ups, speaking in an unfamiliar accent Ysolda had heard only once before, from the mouth of the nameless girl. Whoever they were, they were from the Lakes.

Fear set her teeth on edge, but there was excitement too. It was hardly common for people from the Lakes to cross into Glaw Wood, so in all likelihood they were

Ryders. And Hari could be with them. Ysolda slowed her pace to a snail's, sinking lower and lower to the ground until she was crawling.

They had set up camp in a hollow, edged by the risen remains of a long-abandoned badger sett. The level of their voices suggested they were not worried about, nor expecting to be overheard. Ysolda was able to crawl right to the other side of the sett and listen.

'You're sure these are edible?' said an imperious woman's voice. 'I still think we should try the red ones. They're everywhere.'

'If the birds have left them we definitely should,' replied a man's.

'Still, I don't like the look of these.' An audible sniff.

The hairs on Ysolda's arms stood on end. She dared not sneak a look, but was certain they were Ryders. As if to confirm her suspicions, she heard the snicker of a horse.

'Shut up, both of you,' said another woman, softer but more authoritative. 'There's an easy way to work out if they're safe.'

The sound of a branch snapping beneath a heavy boot. Ysolda shrank lower to the curve of the hill, and looked up, able to see Nara in the tree above her and the top of a head. Black hair, braided with silver. The flash of a crimson cloak. Ysolda's whole body shook with her heartbeat.

The woman was walking around the smoking fire to

the horses. Ysolda inched higher so she could watch her, bargaining on her companions doing the same. The clearing was ringed by rowan and young birches. Ysolda could see they'd snapped back the saplings for their fire, and the broken trees were oozing sap. All three of the adults wore red cloaks, their black hair worn long and looped into a braid with silver thread. The walking woman wore a necklet of beaten silver, the tips of her hair wrapped in amber beads. She was clearly in charge.

The horses stood at the opposite side from Ysolda, and as the soft-voiced woman approached, they whinnied slightly. There was a whip at the woman's side, but she used it open to push apart the horses and step between them. She was broad shouldered, so Ysolda could not see past her, but she heard a whimper.

She froze, holding her breath. Was it Hari?

She moved around the ring of the clearing, a small dip where the sett had collapsed offering a better view. She could see two shapes slouched on the ground beside the horses, their arms oddly raised. They were tied by their wrists to the horses' saddles.

The soft-voiced woman stood over them, nudging the smaller shape with her boot. It shifted, the meagre firelight hitting his face. A boy, perhaps Ysolda's age. His brown skin was shiny with tears.

'Open wide,' said the woman, bending to him. In her

hand, she held a palmful of small white berries. Even from this distance, Ysolda recognised them as mistletoe. Two thoughts wrestled for attention in her mind – why mistletoe, now, at the end of summer? Like the beechnuts and rowan berries, they were working to a strange timing. And they were poisonous.

The boy clenched his lips together, but the woman squeezed his cheeks. Ysolda heard his jaw pop.

'Leave him,' said another voice, and the larger shape resolved into an old Lakes woman, hair white and eyes misty, but she turned them fiercely on to the rider. 'I'll taste them.'

'We need a faster test than your old body allows,' said the Ryder. She still didn't raise her voice, but its softness was a feather lure concealing a hook. 'Come on, boy.'

Ysolda hesitated a moment. If she sat here and did nothing, the boy would fall gravely ill. Perhaps he would die and she could have prevented it. But Hari wasn't here, and if she revealed herself there was no telling what the Ryders would do to her.

She searched the trees for Nara, wondering if she could signal to the hawk to swoop in and knock the berries from the rider's palm. But Nara was fixated on the shadows beneath her perch, searching for a late-night snack.

The Ryder had pushed aside the old woman and was bending low over the boy, forcing his mouth open.

The other two were laughing, and a roar sounded in Ysolda's ears. She picked up a stone and fitted it into her slingshot. Taking quick and careful aim, she fired at the woman's hands.

It missed, hitting her in the shoulder, but with sufficient force that she exclaimed in pain and spun around, scattering the poisonous berries to the ground. Ysolda stood to run, but her foot caught in an exposed root. She fell, dropping her slingshot and feeling her carefully gathered bullaces and berries squash beneath her.

Terror flooded her, but she had the sense not to fight, reaching for her obsidian blade and thrusting it into her borrowed boot. No sooner had she done this than the two watching Ryders were on her, yanking her roughly to her feet.

CHAPTER TEN

GIFTED

Nara screeched, but Ysolda whistled her off. There was no sense in both of them being caught. She lost sight of the hawk as the male rider yanked her head back by her braid, sneering down at her.

'Who's this?' said the first woman. 'One of your cousins, Cai?'

The man hissed at her as the soft-voiced woman nudged him aside, twining her own long fingers through Ysolda's hair.

'Hello, girl. I did not know Glaw Wood folk could aim.' She rubbed the place the stone had struck her. Cai scooped up Ysolda's slingshot and threw it to his taunting companion. She sniffed at it and threw it on to the fire. Ysolda whimpered as her hair pulled, watching her hand-carved weapon go up in spluttering smoke.

'Primitive weapon.'

'Now, Ani. No need to be rude,' said the soft-voiced woman. Up close, she was a mass of even more confusing contradictions. Her skin was smooth and glowed tawny gold in the firelight, the black of her hair almost blue, like a raven's wing. Her eyes were large and dark brown, ringed with long lashes – she should have been beautiful. But there was something detached about her gaze. 'Do you speak?'

Ysolda opened her mouth, but only a squeak came out. She had never been so scared. The woman reached into her mouth and pinched her tongue, laughing as Ysolda squirmed. She let go of her, and Ysolda tried to back out of the clearing, but Ani and Cai were behind her, spears drawn.

'Well, General?'

Through her panic, Ysolda realised they were waiting for an order.

'Are you gifted, girl?' said the general.

Ysolda shook her head, wincing as strands of hair snapped.

'Shame.' She nodded to the waiting Ryders. Too late, Ysolda realised she had damned herself. They raised their blades, ready to strike—

'Wait!' She threw up her palm, coming so close to the

spear tip she could feel the cool of the steel. 'I am not gifted, but I have something you need.'

'How do you know what we need?' asked the general.

'It's a Glaw Wood trick, General,' said Ani dismissively, her spear now pressed against Ysolda's palm. Ysolda felt the warm trickle of blood.

'The End-World Wood,' said Ysolda. 'I know where it is.'

The general motioned to Ani, who lowered her spear reluctantly. 'Who told you about the End-World Wood?'

'We all know it,' said Ysolda possessively. 'Our Elder Alder is the southernmost tree of that ancient forest.'

'We have scouts on their way there at this very moment,' said Ani.

'To the Kalti Forest?' said Ysolda. 'That is not where it lies.'

'So?' said Ani. 'We will track it down sooner or later.'

'How do you know all this?' said the general, narrowing her eyes suspiciously. 'Are you gifted after all?'

'Only born of Glaw Wood,' said Ysolda, more bravely than she felt. 'Our trees are intricately linked.'

'Tell us then, girl,' said the general, pushing Ysolda to the ground, dark eyes fixed on her. 'Where is it?'

Ysolda opened her mouth, but the old woman tied to the horse made a small gesture, and Ysolda hesitated. Her conversation with the strange girl was a bargaining chip –

an opportunity. Ysolda had to think how best to use it, and an idea arrived sudden as the quake.

Lakes people were famous for their superstitions, their beliefs in systems Ysolda had no idea of. But then they probably had no idea about those of Glaw Wood. She lifted her chin and in the dirt, her hands clenched. This would be the tell, the sign Hari would look for to tell her Ysolda was lying – but these people did not know her. She was a good liar to all but Hari.

'I cannot tell you.'

Ani laughed hollowly, and held the spear back up, this time to Ysolda's throat. 'I think you can.'

Ysolda tried not to shake, to hold the general's unflinching gaze with the same intensity. 'It's not that I'm not willing. But none of us could speak it. The knowledge is bone-known – if we tried, our tongues would latch to our teeth, our jaw would clench, and we would fall to the ground unable to say a word.'

It sounded ridiculous even to Ysolda, and she hoped the general would not expect a demonstration. But instead of disbelief, a flicker of recognition passed between the Ryders.

'Like the Forgiver's attacks,' murmured Cai.

'But she is not an oracle,' said Ani. 'Only a Glaw Wood dweller.'

Ysolda's fists clenched tighter. 'Only a Glaw Wood

dweller could lead someone there. You could look and look and never find it else.'

'She may be lying,' said Ani, but she did not sound as sure. Then Ysolda saw the moment when the general decided to believe her.

'We've seen stranger things,' said the general. 'There was that quake that took a horse, further west. They have the girl that caused it in hand.'

Ysolda's scalp crawled. They were talking about Hari, they must be. But Hari hadn't summoned the quake.

'Besides, Seren can decide what is the truth.'

She nodded at Cai, who drew a length of rope from his horse's saddlebag. Ani seized Ysolda's shoulder roughly, and together the Ryders tied her hands to the third horse.

Ysolda was able to sit, but barely, with her arms raised above her head. The smell of the horse was warm and sweet as cut grass, and soothed her racing heart a little. The Ryders grumbled, searching for the forgotten mistletoe berries.

'Those are poisonous,' said Ysolda, unwilling to watch them try to force the boy to eat them again. 'Eat the rowans.'

'Rowans?'

She gestured with her chin to the canopy of red berries.

'After you,' said Ani, picking a handful and stuffing them into Ysolda's mouth. She chewed and swallowed. The Ryders waited a few moments, and seemed to decide the signs would have shown themselves. Ysolda knew they wouldn't have, but still she was glad of her mouthful of tart berries, tasting of home, of safety, of everything that felt – and was – so many miles away at that moment.

When the Ryders had settled at the fire again, the old woman whispered, 'Fast thinking. I'm sorry I forced the lie but I couldn't see them kill you.'

'It may be worse, what's awaiting us,' murmured the boy mournfully.

'Hush, Sami. Don't speak like that.'

'Thank you for helping me,' said Ysolda.

'It was not much,' sighed the old woman. 'Once I could have called an animal to distract them, but they're making us wear these.' She pointed, as best she could, to her chest. Ysolda saw an amulet made of an uneven, silvery material tied to a leather cord, like the one she now wore. 'Fool's gold. It mists our abilities. And I am tired. Maybe Sami would have been more use.'

'The amulet is sapping me too. I doubt I could call a breeze right now.'

'You can summon weather?'

'Cold weather,' he said.

'There are no animals to call, anyway. No squirrels, no birds.' The woman shivered. 'It feels wrong here. Is Glaw Wood always so empty?'

Ysolda shook her head before realising she couldn't see her. 'No. You're from the Lakes?'

'For our sins. I'm Deepti,' said the woman. 'This is Sami.'

'I was only born there,' said the boy defensively. 'I didn't choose it.'

'Nor did I,' said the old woman sharply. 'I was brought from the queen's third court. I was a tea grower – it suited my abilities with plants and animals. A world away.'

Ysolda's belly tightened. 'You're a servant?'

Deepti winced. 'I did not choose to serve such a woman. But she was not always cruel. I did not always feel so unsafe, as a green-touch.'

'That's what you call it, what you do?'

'Yes. It is not so uncommon, where I am from. It's not magic, only sensing, encouraging.'

'I understand,' said Ysolda. 'My sister Hari, she hears trees. We call it listening.'

'Is she—'

'Taken by the Ryders, yesterday.'

'I'm sorry—'

A raucous shout of laughter from the Ryders, and the woman fell silent a moment. 'Do you really know where the End-World Wood is?'

'Yes,' said Ysolda.

'That is precious information. Keep it close. The queen has become obsessed with finding it, collecting any gifted who may be able to help. I knew it wasn't safe. Sami and I work in the kitchen gardens. We picked our moment,' she continued, in a lower voice. 'We tried to run, reached what we thought was safety in these woods. We did our best.'

Sami's voice was mournful. 'It wasn't enough.'

CHAPTER ELEVEN

LEAVES

The Ryders kept up a merciless pace. They could easily have allowed their prisoners to ride with them – the horses were broad backed, far bigger than any pony Ysolda had ever seen, and standing higher than her head – but the Ryders seemed to enjoy the sport of watching them stumble behind, losing their footing. They clearly were in less of a hurry than Ysolda had supposed them to be, breaking at dusk the next day to make another camp, sleeping past sunrise.

Unbound on foot, Ysolda could have just about kept up. The forest path was narrow, Ani or Cai frequently dismounting to hack a wider route with their fearful metal spears, and this prevented the horses from going at breakneck speed. But still it was fast enough to keep Ysolda in a constant terror of falling, of her shoulders being wrenched from their sockets. She was amazed Deepti could walk so fast – yes, she was taller than either Sami or she, but the woman was older than most reached in Glaw Wood, and her wrists were narrow as a sapling's first growth.

Sami made the most fuss, crying and tripping frequently. He'd wept all night too, Ysolda sleeping in snatches and waking to his sobs. She wished she could soothe him, but what was there to say? Besides, he knew better than she what awaited them – perhaps she should be crying too. Her greatest comfort was Nara, swooping occasionally overhead, appearing through gaps in the canopy, wide brown wings pinned out against the grey, forbidding sky.

The Ryders at least did seem to want to keep them alive. They fed them more berries in the early morning, gave them mouthfuls of stale water Ysolda knew were from stagnant pools. They passed mossy banks, trunks rich with edible mushrooms, and Ysolda wondered about telling them they were passing springs where water was cool and abundant, but she did not want to speak to them any more than necessary.

When the Ryders stopped at midday, passing around a flatbread topped with a sweet-smelling butter, Nara alighted in a tall yew. Ysolda longed to feel her comforting weight on her shoulder, the snap of her beak in her ear. But so long as Nara was free, a part of Ysolda was free too, and that made her less afraid.

'Here,' she murmured, nudging Sami's foot with her own. Ysolda pointed out a hawthorn next to where the horses were tethered, indicating they could eat the leaves. They dared not talk openly with the Ryders so close by, and Sami looked sceptical, but his eyes soon closed in delight after his first bite. He passed some across to Deepti, and Ysolda slid more into her belt. She did not know when the Ryders might allow them to eat again.

Ysolda leaned her forehead against the hawthorn, chewing the tangy leaves until they broke down into a familiarly comforting mush. It was a young tree still, perhaps fifty years old. Her heart panged as she wondered when the wood would end. It would not be much further – they were far beyond anything she knew and the wolf queen's bounds bit at the borders of Glaw Wood. She remembered the map drawn in the dirt by the stranger with a Ryder's spear – the thin lines breaking apart the world from everything she knew. She eyed Ani's weapon where it lay by her side.

Though the Ryder had mocked Ysolda's slingshot as primitive, easily broken, they didn't seem to realise that this was the point. The people of Glaw Wood took only what they needed, built things that could break and be mended, or else be returned to the soil as ash. The Lakes people though – they wanted monuments. They built henges of stone and forged blades of steel. It was as though they were afraid to be forgotten, as if forgetting were not the whole point of a life cycle.

Ysolda took another bite of hawthorn leaf, eyeing Sami. He was watching his feet, his hands swollen from being tied so long. She should not really blame ordinary Lakes people, she knew. It was the wolf queen's invaders that changed the land. And even then she knew there were many like Deepti, who had not come fully of their own will.

The Ryders and their queen then – that is where Ysolda should aim her hatred, her fear. It was easily done, with her fingers tingling numbly in their bonds, with Hari taken away from her.

Cai belched. 'On then.'

The general was staring at the sky thoughtfully. 'I think we should saddle them.' She jerked her head at Ysolda and the others. 'Looks like a storm coming, and the forest breaks soon.'

Cai wrinkled his nose but Ani nodded and untied Deepti, pulling her roughly to her feet. 'Up.' It was clear Deepti did not have the strength to haul herself on to the horse. Ani shoved her. 'Come on.'

'She can't,' said Ysolda hotly. 'Untie me, I'll help her.'

The general sliced through Ysolda's ropes, looking her

dead in the eye. 'Don't try anything.'

Ysolda hadn't considered it, but the moment the ropes fell free she felt light, reckless. She looked up at Nara, poised in the tree. She could run, and run, and maybe they wouldn't catch her. She knew these woods better than them, she trusted the trees to slip her from sight neat as a knife into a sheath. But that would not get her any closer to Hari, or her stolen amulet. So instead she went to the old woman and bent, bracing her hands on her knees so Deepti could stand on her back.

'Are you sure?' whispered the woman, and Ysolda nodded. Hari had helped her climb trees like this, but when the woman stepped on to her back, she was light. Too light. Her bones seemed almost hollow.

Even with Ysolda to help, Deepti struggled to swing her leg over the horse, and was panting by the time she sat centrally on the horse's back, behind the cow's-hide saddle. Ani swung herself up in front, her muddy boots scuffing roughly down Deepti's legs.

Sami was forced up behind Cai, and the general tied Ysolda's ropes again. There was something softer in her gaze. 'How old are you, girl?'

'Thirteen.'

'My daughter is thirteen. I wonder if she is taller than you.'

'Where is she?'

The softness vanished. 'Up.'

Ysolda had never sat on a horse so high. She could feel the animal's power, and also its fear. Seren did not ride a horse, the stories went, but a sea wolf big as a bear. What must that be like?

The general swung herself up. Ysolda didn't know where to hold on, and when the general kicked the horse into action she was forced to hook her fingers through the woman's belt to keep from falling. The leather was soft and supple, somehow repellent. But Ysolda had to hold on, and the general didn't stop her. Her spear wound was already healing, though it still stung her palm to hold so tightly.

The end of the wood came as a shock. There was none of the usual petering out, like at the coast, where the trees shifted from hawthorn and yew to hardy rowans and pines, trees that could anchor themselves against storms in sandy soil, could wrap their roots about rocks and cling through the fiercest winds. The wood simply stopped in its tracks, like a halted army.

It caught Nara by surprise too, and she swooped into sight for the first time, continuing on over their heads. Before them was unlike anything Ysolda had ever seen. There were hills stripped of trees and sown with crops. A silvery lake shimmered at the base of their vantage point, and a wide crossroads had been beaten into the dust, one track running straight ahead into an endless distance, another intersecting it left to right across the Ryders' path.

The Ryders turned left, north. Ysolda knew from warning stories the wolf queen's castle stood at the coast. Would it be just as Hari had said, built of the wrecks of the wolf queen's conquests?

The wind was fierce without the tree cover, and Ysolda cowered in the general's shadow, clinging on tightly as the horse bore her away from everything she knew, towards a fabled queendom. Towards Hari.

CHAPTER TWELVE

RED SKY

With nothing to impede their way, the Ryders whipped the horses into a gallop, the general's red cloak batting Ysolda's face. She threw off a scent of heather and a deep spice, almost peppery. It was as different from sap and moss as it was possible to be, and Ysolda's stomach gave a tangible tug of homesickness, the cord binding her to Glaw Wood straining. Her legs ached from clinging to the horse, and she checked as often as she could on Deepti, the old woman's lined face grim and closed with pain.

The horses seemed to fly across the compacted ground, but soon the wind picked up. It became a gale, alternately speeding and impeding the horses, who trembled as the sky took on an ominous charge. Nara was flung on invisible currents, flying further and further to the left of them, where Ysolda knew the sea must be.

They were racing the storm, and they lost. The hairs on Ysolda's arms stood up, and she thought she felt the general shiver too as they rode between the valley of two hills and out on to a broader track of whitish limestone lined with high, silvery grasses.

The horses' hooves kicked up a fine dust that stuck in Ysolda's throat, and she stifled coughs in her shoulder. The air itself was heavy and thick with promised thunder, and as Ysolda spotted the grey sea that bordered the Lakes at its western edge, the first streak of lightning licked the sky.

Cai's horse gave a whinny and sidestepped, its distress swallowed a moment later by the roll of thunder. Sami cried out and must have tightened his grip on Cai, because a moment later he grunted as the rider elbowed him in the ribs. But it was clear the Ryders were not as in control as they wanted to appear.

The wind intensified. The three horses were set against the teeth of its current now, pushing hard, slowed almost to a walk. The storm was nearly over their heads, and Ysolda looked up at the thickening clouds. They were all wrong. Her mouth fell open, and was immediately filled with grit.

The clouds were lit red, red as sap, as fresh blood. Ysolda had never seen such a bright sky so dark in its intent. It did not look right. It did not look natural.

'What the—' exclaimed Ani, but the woman's words were snatched by a simultaneous flash of lightning and grumble of thunder. The storm was on top of them now, clamping down like a flaming cage. Despite herself, Ysolda dug in closer to the general's back. The general kicked her horse's sides, but the creature was clearly terrified.

'To the bank,' shouted the general above the roar of the storm and led her animal crosswise to a narrow overhang of granite, ridged as a spine, holding the hill back from the road. They had to press themselves flat to fit underneath, the general lying across her horse's neck. Everything glowed a malevolent crimson, and Ysolda let her terror sweep her along, squeezing her eyes shut and burrowing her face into the general's cloak, but that was red too – the whole world was red and red and blood pounding in her ears—

Suddenly, Ysolda's breath became audible. Ragged gasps, like she'd been running. The pressure in her ears was gone, the charge that sparked the air vanished. It was like being dropped from a fierce grip, her ribcage expanding freely again.

The storm had passed. It had lasted only a few minutes.

With a cluck of her tongue, the general led them out of the overhang. Ysolda scanned the sky for Nara, but the hawk was nowhere in sight. The red clouds had gone, scooped along by the wind, and overhead were left white, wispy rakes, like mighty claws rending the grey sky.

'What in Seren's name was that?' exclaimed Ani.

'It was just a storm,' snapped the general. 'Don't lose your head, Ani.'

'But there was no rain, and that red sky!' Ani shuddered. Behind her, Deepti's face was creased in concern, and behind Cai, Sami's face was pallid. Clearly none of them had ever seen anything like it.

'Do you think they saw it at the castle?' asked Cai.

'I'm certain they did,' said the general. 'She has sent us an escort.'

The woman was looking further up the road, and her carefully impassive face was shadowed a moment by worry. Ysolda followed her gaze, and again a chill entered her blood. Ahead, black against the white limestone of the road, were five large shapes moving at an incredible speed.

Cai swore, and the general recovered herself, raising her chin defiantly at the gaining forms. At first Ysolda thought they were riderless horses free of saddles or reins, but they were too low to the ground, their gait more focused and compact, like arrows skimming the road.

'Wolves,' she said, the realisation escaping her mouth as a gasp.

'Sea wolves,' corrected the general. 'Her wolves.'

They were huge. The closer they got, the less they made sense, built like the wolves that stalked Glaw Wood and terrorised the deer and boars, but with thicker pelts and larger legs, their colours becoming more apparent the closer they got – and oh! how fast they came, like nightmares covering ground – coats lightening into shades of grey and white, their muzzles bright behind the black smears of their noses.

They were barely a head shorter than the horses, tall as the pony Gwen used to take to the sea to help dig out peat, the one Ysolda used to ride when she was younger and it seemed the highest place in the world, on that pony's back.

The horse whinnied, and the general had to dig in her heels to make it move towards the approaching wolves. Ysolda could sense the animal's unwillingness, an elemental resistance. They progressed in convoy, Ysolda twisting in the saddle to glimpse the others following, Cai and Ani struggling to keep their horses at a canter.

Finally, they reached the wolves. The animals did not break their stride, only slowed and swirled around them, two at either side and one at the rear. Something instinctive in Ysolda shrivelled up, like a dead leaf. She had nothing against wolves – in Glaw Wood they were part of the system, the natural order that kept everything in balance. But these were not like Glaw Wood wolves.

Aside from their size and their colouring, there was an unmistakable restraint to them. They were trained, and all of it was against their nature. No Glaw Wood wolf would escort horses instead of attack them. No Glaw Wood wolf would fall into step with its companions like a battalion of soldiers. No Glaw Wood wolf would study her with such sharp intensity. With a wild animal, you knew what you were getting. With Seren's sea wolves, it all felt entirely wrong.

The wolves' backs were level with the horses' bellies, and Ysolda wished she could draw her legs up to her chest. They didn't howl or snap their teeth, but they did keep their eyes on the horses, trotting alongside and emitting low, barely audible growls when the horses hesitated. It was enough to keep them in check and in a state of awful alertness.

Ysolda was clenching her teeth so hard it hurt. No one spoke, and in the wake of the storm the world seemed unnaturally quiet, only the *clip-clop* of hooves on limestone, the snorts of the horses, the low hum of the wolves' warning rumble.

She was focused on not looking at the animals either side of them, and it took her a moment to notice the silvery grasses had fallen away to their left, leaving a shelving bank of sandy soil that rolled gently to meet the sea. Small waves lapped the brownish sand, and it all seemed so placid, so calm.

At last, Ysolda spotted Nara skimming low over the waves further out. The hawk dived neatly, wings folded to her feathered body, the sea slipping her from view for a moment before she emerged again, flapping to gain height, a silver fish clasped in her beak. With the sea nearby, the same sea that lapped the short beach of Glaw Wood's coast, and Nara safe and fed, Ysolda almost allowed herself to feel hopeful a moment.

But then the wolf to her left snarled briefly, a cut of white fang sharp against its red lip, and she remembered to be afraid.

CHAPTER THIRTEEN

A CASTLE

It appeared like a heat haze, a mirage. A castle, low and sprawling, and more magnificent or strange than anything Ysolda could have imagined.

Its nearness crept up on her, for there were no dwellings dotting the road, no sign that this was the concentration of the wolf queen's power. Instead there were slumped wooden beams lining the route, poles of varying height stuck deep into the sand like rows of gapped teeth.

The road narrowed, forcing two wolves ahead and three behind, and the poles were planted closer and closer together. There seemed to be writing on them, but it wasn't Ogham, nor any language Ysolda recognised, let alone understood. Eventually the beams formed a wall that blocked the sea from view, funnelling Ysolda's gaze ahead as they crested a small dune. She peered around the general, and there it was. Seren's castle.

It stood alone amid dunes long trampled to reveal their limestone beds, so the roads leading to and from the castle looked like limb-bones laid in the sand. *Giants' bones*, thought Ysolda, and the castle itself a mighty ribcage. It was formed of maybe a hundred beached boats, but 'boat' was not a big enough word for what these vessels must have been when they floated.

Ships, whole cities, whole countries: vast numbers of planks moulded into graceful arcs, their upturned hulls sprinkled with barnacles and raised on stilts made of their own masts, their sails pulled between to form huge canvas walls, so taut they barely rippled. As the wind shifted Ysolda caught its scent on the breeze: salt and rot, the unpleasant undercurrent of long-dredged things and bitter black sea mud.

Shapes moved across the gigantic hulls – wolves posted across the surface, keeping watch and presumably stopping gulls from nesting in the castle's many nooks. She remembered why she was here, that she was prisoner, and that somewhere in that vast mass of stinking, defeated ships was Hari.

Hari, forced to listen to the dead wood groaning around her, perhaps stuffed into a tiny space with dozens more gifted or, worse, alone. Ysolda searched for Nara, spotted her worrying a group of gulls bobbing on the grey sea, and the sight made her brave again.

They reached a gate formed of many doors slotted against one another like a woven basket. Some of them still had handles attached, ornately carved, and thick, glinting locks. Some even had deep slashes in the wood, and she wondered if the marks were made before or after they became a gate to guard the wolf queen's castle.

'On,' said the general. Two of their escorting wolves trotted ahead, splitting up either side of the gate. The riders stopped before it, but did not dismount. The wolves were heading to two identical wheels, each with a sharpened stake at their centre. As the wolves stepped into the wheels, two paws before the stake and two after, their bellies a mere inch above the stake's point, Ysolda saw how cruel, how clever the design was. If a person tried to stand in it, they would be impaled. These were designed only for wolves.

As the creatures began to run, turning the wheels, leaping clear of the stakes, the gate creaked open, lifted on an invisible pulley system. A waft of warm salty air washed over them, but Ysolda couldn't see what lay beyond – it was gloomy inside. The general squeezed the horse's sides with her heels, leading them into the mouth of the wolf queen's castle.

'Home sweet home,' said Ani.

They entered a high-ceilinged courtyard of sorts, canvas on two sides and the gate behind, massive double doors the height of the room before them. Feeble light shone down through meagre gaps in the structure. Along one canvas wall horses were tied to a hollowed trunk serving as a trough. Ryders in crimson cloaks strode across the space interspersed with dark-clothed men and women, who seemed to be servants like Deepti and Sami and trailed behind the Ryders carrying spears or equipment for them and their horses. These people were white as she, or brown-skinned, but the Ryders were all dark as the general.

No torches illuminated the space, and it all felt murky and underwater. Even the sound seemed submerged, Ryders calling to one another and horses snickering. Ysolda was relieved to see the wolves remained outside, and there were none in here.

The general rode to the trough and two men hurried to take the reins. 'Hold her,' the general told one, and Ysolda was roughly grappled from the horse to the ground, held tightly by the wrists. She tried to look the man in the face, but he kept his gaze turned determinedly away. The general dismounted and took hold of Ysolda herself, and beside them Cai and Ani took charge of Sami and Deepti too.

'Stop gawping, girl. There's more to come.' The general pushed Ysolda before her to the massive pair of doors. Four servants heaved on them, two to each, and they swung inwards, revealing another vaulted space thronged with people. The sounds spilled out, languages Ysolda didn't know, smells of cooking.

Cai and Ani had drawn level and Ysolda glanced at their hostages. Deepti was ashen, and Sami shiny with sweat. Ysolda frowned. What was affecting them so badly?

Then she remembered the amulets around their necks. The fool's gold, sapping them of their gift. It must feel horrible. She shuddered, wondering if Hari had to wear one too.

They were pulled forward into the room. Here were men, women and children who did not seem to be servants or Ryders, talking and trading from long tables stacked with dried seaweed and fish, powders and crystals like the kind on the gifteds' amulets. They wore a mesh of styles – long tunics over leggings, smocks belted at the waist, their hair braided with silver like the general's. Their clothes were dyed in colours Ysolda had never seen before: egg-yolk yellow, shimmering blue. Among the languages Ysolda did not understand were words she did, landing on her ears like thrown kindnesses.

'Trout, mackerel!'

'Firewood!'

'Silver, steel, amber!'

The mention of amber twisted her stomach and she felt an almost physical absence against her chest, the amulet travelling further and further from Glaw Wood, where it belonged.

Their group brushed through the crowd, the general cutting an easy path, people standing aside for her and staring with open curiosity at Ysolda, who stared with open curiosity back. The space was wider than the one they had just left, and had a more solid feeling to it. There were no gaps in the ceiling, and again no torches, but the whole place was suffused with a blueish-white glow. Ysolda could not immediately tell where it was coming from, but then, through a natural break in the throng, she noticed another wooden trough lining the edges of the space. It was full of water, and in it, something glowed.

Many things, minute as flies, seemed to swim in their millions, emitting a strange, ghostly light, like a beam of early morning sun cutting through a shutter. She saw two children splashing the water at each other while their fathers chatted nearby, and it was like their hands were full of crystals that shone softly anywhere the water fell.

Ysolda wished she could get closer, see what exactly it was, but the general's grip was firm and her pace unrelenting. The crowd closed around the troughs, and Ysolda turned her attention to the ceiling high above. The light from the trough was carried up the wooden walls by glimmering nails that seemed to be made of quartz, hammered in at regular intervals to reflect the glow. Still, it could not illuminate the uppermost reaches, and she shuddered. It was like being underground, or submerged in the belly of a ship, floating out on a vast and uncertain sea.

'Close your mouth, I told you,' said the general. 'She does not like gawking.'

They stopped before another set of doors, smaller but still standing high above their heads. These were of a different sort of wood, silvery as birch. It looked like it had been stained with dye, and engraved into these doors was an image of a wolf flanked by two spears crossed over its snarling head. The wolf's eyes were inlaid with amber and glowed red in the pale light.

A thrill of fear shivered through her. She had thought they would be taken to wherever the gifted were being held. She did not feel ready to face the wolf queen.

'Search her,' the general ordered Ani.

Ani roughly felt Ysolda's clothes, pulling out hawthorn leaves, moss, and the gut thread with a derisive snort. Ysolda held her breath, waiting for her to find the obsidian in her boot, but Ani barely bothered to bend. 'All clear, General.'

The general knocked twice on the doors, and the sound echoed around them, hushing the high room. The doors swung open.

CHAPTER FOURTEEN

THE HULL HALL

It was a chamber of many doors, the smallest of the three rooms they had come to, and the most impressive. Formed from a single ship's hull, its floor mimicked the eye-shape of the walls, coming to a point at the left and a straight line to the right. The floor was formed of wood, but the planks had been carved to echo the curves, creating concentric rings that tightened around a central throne, beside which two servants stood, both silent and watchful. Mercifully, the throne itself was empty, but the whole room tingled with expectation.

Ysolda looked around. The straight wall was entirely given over to an enormous map. It was brightly painted in pigments Ysolda had never seen before, rich sky blue and Mabon-leaf yellows, and showed a world far bigger than

Ysolda recognised. From her memory of the stranger's spear-scratched map she could identify the Isles, with the Lakes and Kalti lands and Suthridge marked, but they were dwarfed by sea – so much sea, so much blue, Ysolda felt dizzy.

She searched for the End-World Wood, but its tidal island was not marked, or else too small to be of notice. There was Norveger, the mountainous land of the Norse, and the Marbled Hills to the south, the Thawless Circle to the north. The latter was stitched about in gold, as was much of the map Ysolda realised, now she had studied it longer. The wolf queen's realms, portioned off.

'Stand there.' The general steered Ysolda closer, until the six of them stood in front of the throne. It too was built of wreckage, treated like the finest materials. Both the floor and the throne were studded with crystals, some Ysolda recognised – black obsidian, pink rose quartz, greenish topaz – and some she did not, in vibrant shades of yellow and blue.

These had the effect of throwing the eye, not letting it settle anywhere. Everywhere was glinting colour and different textures of wood and stone, and as in the previous room, light-filled troughs lined the walls, but these spiralled upwards too, so every inch of the room was lit by the tiny glowing creatures. There was nowhere to hide.

She refocused on the map in an effort to distract herself.

There was another order to it, now she stood closer. Faint silver stitches, less bold than the gold of the wolf queen's realms, criss-crossing like spiderwebs through countries and oceans. One line ran from Glaw Wood to the Lakes, up through the Kalti Forest to where the End-World Wood should be, and on to Norveger, where a mighty mountain was marked in deepest black.

'Stay still,' snapped the general, and Ysolda realised she must have been leaning closer to the map in an effort to make sense of it. 'She'll be here soon.'

Ysolda watched the encircling doors with a feeling like sickness in her belly. Which would the wolf queen emerge from? Would she really be as terrifying as the stories said? Ysolda imagined fangs and hair matted with blood, sharp fingernails like talons.

Directly behind the throne, a door opened. The servants stood straighter. The seat of crystal and wrecks obscured Ysolda's vision, but she felt the hairs on her arms rise as a heavy padding drew closer.

When the wolf queen rounded the throne, Ysolda gasped aloud, the general's grasp painful on her shoulder. Seren was exactly as the stories told – a monster with the head of a woman and the body of a wolf.

But then the illusion dissolved. Seren was on the back of an enormous sea wolf, bigger than those that had escorted them. She rode without saddle or reins, legging-clad calves hanging either side of the massive animal. Her hair was loose, falling in a thick, waist-length sheet of deepest black, strands of silver coiling through it.

And though the general was beautiful, the wolf queen's looks were awe-full. It was a terrible sort of beauty – like looking at a goddess. Her skin shone a deep, deep bronze, and her eyes, amber and strangely familiar, were cool as the obsidian blade pressed to Ysolda's ankle.

'You're gawping,' hissed the general.

The queen dismounted in a fluid movement, swinging herself lightly down before the throne. She was within an arm's reach. Ysolda was trembling, but she couldn't control herself. She had never been so scared in all her life.

'Raani,' said the general, reaching out to touch Seren's feet, which Ysolda noticed were bare and painted with an ornate red pattern, like the woad Gwyn had used on his wedding day.

'Queen,' said Seren sharply. 'Remember where we are.'

Ysolda glanced at Deepti and Sami. Both were shaking visibly, Sami crying softly. The queen ascended the steps to her throne, giving a brief command Ysolda couldn't hear. There was no flash of wolfish incisors from her mouth – so that, too, was a myth. The wolf slumped down by the throne, huge as a horse and placid as a pet.

'Three?' said Seren, melodiously low. 'Only two ran

from our halls. I thought when I heard there were three that maybe you'd found . . . But I was mistaken.'

Her voice was a mix of accents, their own dialect and something else. For the first time, Ysolda wondered why Seren spoke their language and had a name that belonged in this country, when she came from so far away.

'We found another, Raan— I mean, Queen,' said the general, nudging Ysolda forward so she stood only inches from the reclining wolf, its thick belly-fur splayed. 'Attacked us in the wood.'

'I did not—' started Ysolda, but Seren raised an eyebrow and Ysolda fell silent.

'What is she?'

'Not gifted, Queen.'

The queen cocked her head. 'Then why did you not get rid of her?'

The general reached suddenly for Ysolda, who flinched, but the woman only pushed her a little ahead towards the throne. 'She's from Glaw Wood. She says she knows where the Anchorite is.'

The queen's full gaze landed like a heavy blow on Ysolda's face. 'Is that so?'

'No,' squeaked Ysolda. She'd never said she knew where the mythical ancient girl was, only the End-World Wood.

The queen sighed. 'Very well.' Her disappointment seemed genuine, but already her gaze was sliding from

Ysolda on to Deepti and Sami. She clicked her fingers once, twice, and the wolf heaved itself to its feet and stared down at Ysolda, something wild slipping beneath its dead eyes. The general stepped back and turned her face away. With an awful certainty, Ysolda realised Seren had ordered her death.

'No!' Ysolda heard Deepti's shout from a great distance. Her heartbeat was furious in her ears, her fingers and toes numb as she looked back at the creature looming over her.

Its growl reverberated through her entire body, its lips lifting to reveal white fangs long as Ysolda's hand. She imagined them plunging into her chest, imagined her blood spilling out across the wood-and-crystal floor. She would never see Hari again, never touch the damp mosses and shining leaves of Glaw Wood. Never feel the weight of Nara landing on her shoulder, or the warming taste of goose pie—

'Wait!' Her own shout came so loud it shocked even Ysolda. Seren paused.

'I know where the End-World Wood is. And that is where you believe the Anchorite to be.'

Seren's eyes narrowed. 'How do you know what I believe?'

For a moment, Ysolda hesitated. She had no loyalty to the thief she'd met in the wood. But still—

'A girl,' she said hesitantly. 'I met her, in the wood.

She . . .' Ysolda's voice failed under the intensity of the queen's glare.

'What did she look like, this girl?'

'She wore a Ryder's cloak, and carried a Ryder's spear. But she looked—' Ysolda's realisation was sudden and sickening. 'Like . . .'

'Me?' murmured the queen.

'Yes,' said Ysolda.

She had never heard of the queen having a child before. But now she was looking directly at Seren's face and in her mind's eye overlaid the face of the stranger. The intensity, the amber eyes, the imperious lift of the lips and the strong chin – she was exactly the wolf queen in miniature. The stranger was Seren's daughter.

CHAPTER FIFTEEN

OATH

The queen and her general exchanged tense glances.

'Why did you not mention this?' said the general. 'What did she tell you?'

Ysolda knew for the stranger's sake she should not say, but the girl would be in no danger, not from her own mother – and Ysolda was in imminent peril. 'That the Anchorite lives in the End-World Wood. And that you believe the forest to be in the mid-north, in the Kalti lands, but that's not right.'

'How do you know this?'

'The Anchorite seeded our Elder Alder, planted at its counterpoint. It's a story we are all told from childhood.' Ysolda didn't mention that it was only that: a story.

'So where is it rooted?'

Ysolda forced herself to meet Seren's eye. Dare she? 'I can't speak it.'

'I order you to.'

'My queen,' said Ysolda, mimicking the general's humble tones. 'I would tell you, but I cannot. An ancient magic holds my tongue.'

Her heart thudded in her ears. It still sounded ridiculous, and the queen would surely realise it was a lie. But the Lakes people were superstitious, with their worship of the sun and moon and henges and monuments, and they believed Glaw Wood to be a primitive place. Perhaps it would work.

'Go on.'

Ysolda's brain rattled, and she readopted a hushed voice. 'I should not say. We are told not to tell anyone beyond our bounds. But, Queen, I do want to help you. If I could tell you outright, I would. When we are born, the secret place is already known like a seed within us, but the knowledge is latched tight to our tongues.

'Think of how a bird follows invisible paths in the air each winter. So we hold the path to the End-World Wood in our hearts. But if I tried to tell you, I would lose my voice. If I tried to draw it for you on a map, my hand would spasm. It is physically impossible.'

'So Thane Boreal will not know,' said the queen as an aside to the general, who made a noise of agreement. 'And you did not tell Eira?'

'Eira?' The stranger, her daughter. *Eira*. Too lovely a name for such a devious person. 'I could not, of course,' and, letting her dislike have full voice, 'nor did I want to.'

The queen laughed at that, and the general glanced at her in shock. She clearly did not laugh often. 'Yes, it was my daughter you met. She has that effect on people. Did she say why she was in Glaw Wood, why she was seeking the Anchorite?'

Ysolda thought a moment, before deciding on the truth. 'She said she wanted to warn them that you were coming. The gifted.'

'And did she say why I sought them?'

Ysolda shook her head. She did not mention the amber amulet, the map the girl had drawn in the dirt.

Seren sat back in her throne of broken boats and mined crystals. 'She is a liar, my daughter. That is something you must know. She did not wish to warn anyone, only defy me. All she does is motivated by selfishness and spite.' She regained her composure, straightening her spine. 'However, I am a woman of my word. And I give you my oath that if you lead me to the Anchorite, I will free you.'

'Not only me,' said Ysolda, trying to contain the tremor in her voice. 'My sister.'

Seren's eyes drifted over Deepti, confused. Shame welled in Ysolda. She had not even thought to bargain for the old woman's and Sami's freedom.

'You have her already. She was taken from the Rhyg.'

'The rift?' said the queen, with interest. 'The tree-listener girl in the stone house? She called a quake, did she not?'

'No,' said Ysolda, dazed that Seren knew such detail about their home. 'She is a listener only. The quake – I don't know why that happened. But Hari would never have called it, even if she could.'

'Another happening, then,' said the queen, almost to herself, but the general nodded.

'Seems it, my queen.'

'Together with the red storm—' Seren trailed her long fingers over the arm of the throne, rubbing a blue stone with her thumb.

'And more, in the woods,' said the general. 'I will tell you all.'

The queen nodded. 'We have little time.'

She stood, so suddenly Ysolda jumped and stumbled back a pace. The queen swung her leg over the wolf and it got to its feet, bringing her high over their heads once more.

'Tomorrow,' she said, eyes already far away. 'You'll lead us to the Anchorite.'

'My queen, it will take many days.'

'On horseback, yes. Wolves are faster.'

'My sister,' said Ysolda, a little desperately. 'I need her to come too—'

'I do not like liars.' Seren's wolf gave a small snarl.

'Not *need*,' corrected Ysolda hastily. 'I mean – please. She's all I have.'

The queen sighed, tapping the wolf between the shoulder blades. It began, slowly, to walk away, back around the throne. 'She is a gifted listener, your sister.'

'Yes,' said Ysolda, shocked the queen knew anything of Hari. But then, she had sent her Ryders to fetch her. 'I know all she knows, of the Anchorite.'

'If that is true,' said Seren, 'then very well.'

Excitement burgeoned in Ysolda's chest.

'When we return, she will be freed.'

Ysolda opened her mouth to argue, to plead for Hari to be freed now, to come with them to the End-World Wood at least, but the general laid a rough, warning hand on her shoulder.

'We'll do the blessing at sunrise,' called the wolf queen over her shoulder. 'Have the Forgiver ready the fires.'

The door banged shut, and it was as though the light in the room spread its focus from the throne to the entire space once more. Deepti gave a deep sigh of relief, and Ysolda's shoulders relaxed slightly.

'Back to the kitchens with them,' the general said to her fellow Ryders. 'Chained, and keep the amulets on.'

Ysolda could not bring herself to meet Deepti's eyes. Sami was glaring at her with open hostility as Cai manhandled him from the Hull Hall, but Deepti said,

'Go well, child,' before Ani shoved her back through the doors out into the wide room. The doors closed behind, leaving the general and Ysolda alone.

The woman wheeled Ysolda around to face her. 'Are you lying, girl?'

'L-Lying?' Ysolda stammered, wishing she could hide her blushes. Her fists curled.

The general's eyes blazed. 'Can you truly lead us to the End-World Wood?'

'Yes.'

'And you encountered her daughter? The girl, Eira, with a stolen cloak and spear?'

'Yes, in Glaw Wood. She looks like her mother. Same eyes, same chin.' *Same haughty expression*, she thought.

The general searched her face and then, seemingly satisfied, loosed Ysolda's shoulders. The skin throbbed. 'You are lucky she did not murder you. The wolf is mercifully quick, but there is no good death for a traitor in this court.'

'Please,' said Ysolda, who knew she was trying her luck. 'May I see my sister?'

'I am not a guide, girl. I will leave you in the gaol, collect you in the morning for our journey.'

'If I could only know she is safe—'

'You are a fool,' said the general, but her voice was not as sharp. 'Didn't I just say I will take you to the gaol?'

Ysolda understood, and fell silent.

'Glaw Wood dolt,' murmured the general, but as she yanked Ysolda towards another door, she could have sworn the woman smiled.

CHAPTER SIXTEEN

HOLD

Dug deep into the compacted sand were steps. They started as wood, presumably salvaged from the conquered ships, but as they left these behind it compressed into stone, the stairs cut from the sand itself, smoothed by many feet.

Here, at last, were torches, set into intervals in the sandstone. Ysolda was glad of their warmth as they descended, her legs shaking, into the leeching cold of the gaol. She wondered if it was only her imagination that set up a roaring in her ears, or whether the sea really was so close, just the other side of one of these gritty walls.

Teeth chattering, she drew closer to the general, who did not pull away. Perhaps it was hopeful thinking, but the woman didn't seem as hardened to her any more. There was the small smile as they had left the Hull Hall, the way she now allowed Ysolda to walk closer by, the previous mention of a daughter her age. But the rough, pinching hold on the back of Ysolda's neck, the tight clasp of the spear in the woman's other hand still suggested otherwise.

After many minutes and many more steps, they reached a door with a small grate set into its middle. Here again, the material of the walls and floor were different, made of some sort of grey bedrock. The general rapped on the door twice with her spear, and a face appeared at the grate. There was the rasping sound of many locks turning and the door swung outwards, releasing a freezing gust of air. It smelled of rotting seaweed, and Ysolda gagged.

The general seemed unaffected and stepped forward into a vaulted cave. The Ryder guarding the door kicked the remains of a meal under a wooden bench, and Ysolda's stomach gurgled. She'd had nothing but hawthorn all day, and even leftovers looked appetising.

'Another gifted,' said the general. 'She's to go with the listeners.'

The general was lying so that Ysolda could go to Hari. The surprise of it made Ysolda blink rapidly as the Ryder gestured for them to follow him, but the general held out her hand. 'I'll take her.'

There was no hesitation from the Ryder – he slid a heavy metal key from his belt and handed it to the general.

Ysolda had never seen a key before – there was no need for them in Glaw Wood, where a leak-proof roof was the only real requirement.

The general pushed her ahead through the cavern. They appeared to be in a series of sea caves, hollowed out far below the beach. The floor was dry but moisture seeped from the walls, and sandflies buzzed angrily around their ankles as they walked a long stone corridor. Hushed whispers came from doors fitted along its length, irregularly shaped to block the mouths of caves. Each was lined with more fool's gold.

They came to a low-hanging space, a lip of rock like the one they'd sheltered under from the storm, beneath which was a door barely wider than the general. There was no grate, but a heavy fool's gold lock was set at its centre. The general bent and spoke through it. 'Stand back.'

A scuffling sound, amplified by the rock, as people scuttled away from the door. Ysolda's heartbeat was loud in her ears. Hari was in there, in this stinking, squashed space. She was about to see her, to hold her.

The general slotted in the key. 'I'll be back for you at sunrise. Try to sleep. There will not be much of that on the road.'

Ysolda didn't know what to say. *Thank you* was all wrong – but she was grateful she was being placed with Hari. She settled on meeting the woman's eyes a moment, but the general looked away, frowning, and pushed open the door.

Darkness pooled at Ysolda's feet. Eyes, bright as woodland creatures, stared into the lit corridor a moment, before the general pushed Ysolda in and closed the door. The key turned, the bolt locked.

Ysolda felt pinioned in place by the blackness, terrified and hopeful. 'Hari?'

There was a panting, nervous silence, and then—

'Ysolda?'

Ysolda's head jolted towards the voice. 'Hari?'

'Ysolda!'

A scrabbling sound as Hari nosed towards her. Ysolda held her arms out in front of her, trying to feel into the darkness, and then she felt a hand on her wrist, icy cold but familiar. Hari pulled her into her arms, and the tears Ysolda had held back since the first, awful moments after the quake spilled over.

She sobbed, and sobbed, and Hari was crying too, her body cold and shaking through her worn clothes. She smelled like everywhere else in these hellish caverns, of rotting and salt and things long buried, but it was Hari, Hari here, alive, holding Ysolda as though she would never let go again.

Their sobs reverberated off the walls, and the others – how many Ysolda didn't know – remained in respectful silence. The world faded away outside Hari's arms, and all Ysolda could feel was relief, the deep relief of sliding into warm woollen sheets after a cold day, the safety and home of it, of her.

But the moment Hari loosened her grip, reality rushed in again. They stayed clutching hands as Ysolda heard others approach.

'This your sister, Hari?' said a man's voice.

'Yes, Uncle,' said Hari. 'But by roots, Ysolda, why? How are you here?'

'I came after you,' said Ysolda, teeth chattering. 'I knew you'd been taken by the Ryders and—'

'I thought you said she wasn't gifted,' said a woman, sounding scared. 'Are they taking others too? Who did you travel with?'

'Two people from the kitchens. Deepti and Sami.'

'Deepti,' said Uncle, sighing. 'I'm surprised she got so far. Almost to the coast?'

'But she is gifted. Are they taking people who aren't? My son—'

'No,' said Ysolda, turning blindly to the voice. 'I lied. I said I was gifted so they'd bring me.'

'Oh, Ysolda,' sighed Hari. 'Why would you do that?'

'To help you,' said Ysolda. 'I couldn't leave you—'

'The thought of you out there was all that gave me hope!' snapped Hari. 'What good is it, the two of us in here?'

Ysolda pulled free, but in the pitch black it was like being on a rocking ship. She stumbled into an unknown figure, who pushed her gently upright. 'I didn't know what else to do! I thought I could help you, could get you out. I still can.'

'There's no way out, child,' said the woman who'd held her up. 'Don't you think we've tried?'

'I'm helping her,' said Ysolda. 'Seren.'

The unseen people held a collective breath.

'What do you mean?' said Uncle. 'Are you her spy?'

'No,' said Ysolda, backing away though she didn't know where he was. 'No, I'm—'

'Helping her?' Hari's voice shook. 'Ysolda, what have you done?'

'She's trying to reach the End-World Wood,' said Ysolda. 'She thought she knew where it was, but she's wrong. I said I'd take her—'

'Why?'

'So she would free you!' Tears started in her eyes again, but they were furious ones, hot and scalding. 'You think I want to help her? I hate her!'

'You really are going?' said the man. 'You will meet with the Forgiver?'

'Yes, at first light. But I don't know who that is.'

'The Forgiver forgives,' said Uncle simply. 'For any sins you will commit on your journey.'

'I won't sin!' shouted Ysolda, her voice bouncing off the walls.

'Hush,' said Hari, and again her sister's arms slipped around her. 'Why does she want to go there?'

Before Ysolda could answer, Uncle's voice issued from the dark. 'The Anchorite,' he said. 'She seeks her?'

'Yes,' said Ysolda. 'But she's just a story, only a myth.'

'No,' said Uncle. 'The Anchorite is real, and if she needs her, things are truly ending.'

'What's ending?'

'Everything.'

CHAPTER SEVENTEEN

WHISPERS

Hari dipped her head to speak into Ysolda's ear. Her breath tickled her cheek. 'Don't listen. They're Lakes people, or else come with Seren from her other realms. They're full to the foreheads with superstitions.'

Though he couldn't have heard, the man spoke as though he had. 'I know you Glaw Wood types think us myth-mad, but you have not seen the things I've seen.'

'Or I,' said the woman. 'I've seen rivers stop flowing and choke red like blood, whales beach themselves on sharp-toothed rocks.'

'I've seen wind rip trees from their roots, lift whole ships and spin them into the air,' said Uncle. 'I've seen lightning strike sideways, and butterflies coat the land like ash.'

Ysolda could tell they were drawing closer, but there

was no threat to it. The darkness made the closeness necessary, and Hari pulled her down into her lap like a young child being rocked to sleep after a nightmare. She had the sensation of being surrounded, the unseen people encircling them like a protective ring, the grunts as they lowered themselves to the cold stone ground.

'We've all seen strangeness, right enough,' said Hari. 'There are places outside this land where my listening is witchcraft, where your growing is thought wrong, Uncle, and your weather reading, Aunty.'

'But these things are natural,' said the woman. 'An ancient girl is no such thing.'

'Because there is no such thing,' said Hari, exasperated.

'You're wrong,' said Uncle. 'And so are you, Aunty. All things on this earth are natural. That is what I'm afraid of. That there is a rightness to it all.'

'All what?' asked Ysolda in a whisper.

'The death,' said Uncle. 'The destruction.'

'Please,' snapped Hari. 'She's just a child.'

'I'm older than you were when you cared for me as a parent,' said Ysolda hotly, but enjoying the hug too much to get off Hari's lap.

'No sense protecting children from words when you can't protect them from the weather,' said Uncle, with the tone of a favourite saying. 'I'm not trying to scare you, child, but I am trying to prepare you. If you really are going with the wolf queen to find the Anchorite, you need to understand this is no make-believe. This is part of something big – bigger than Glaw Wood, or the Lakes, or the seven realms. This is about everything the sky touches, everything the sea soaks, everything the rock –' here he knocked the ground with a muffled thud, and Ysolda guessed he had a walking stick – 'contains. It *is* the sea, the sky, the rock. It's the birds, the animals, the fish. Everything is part of nature, and so is natural.'

'You're talking in riddles,' said Hari dismissively. 'I'm sorry, Uncle, but what is your point?'

Ysolda had never heard Hari speak to an elder this way before. It meant Hari must be afraid, trying to temper the spark of the conversation before it could catch. But too late. Curiosity burned inside her.

Uncle didn't seem concerned by Hari's rudeness. He laughed softly, kindly. 'You sound like my daughter. She would snap her fingers at me and say, *jaldi jaldi*. Hurry, hurry. She acted like there was never enough time. There wasn't, for her.'

'Don't upset yourself, Uncle,' said Aunty. 'But if you are telling this, please tell it straight. This girl needs to know what she's in for.'

'How to begin . . .' said Uncle. 'It is all important. There are many beginnings. Where I am from, it starts with a snake in a bowl of milk—'

The sound of snapping fingers, and Uncle laughed. 'All right, Aunty. Here then, with the wolf queen. You know she hails from my country? That ours was her first realm? And then swathes of the Redlands, the River Jungles, the Marbled Hills – perhaps you have different names for them, but these are what we call them.

'Each place, she adopted a new name. Her first name was Raani, then Thalassa in the Marbled Hills. That's where she found the Forgiver, who there was called an oracle. Now, the queen is Seren. She slips between the places, the names, collecting people and bringing them, seeding them across her realms so she owns them all. She does not merely rule, she inhabits them. Possesses them, truly. At first she was thought merely land hungry, but then there were new whispers. About song lines, dragon lines, ley lines. Have you heard of them?'

Ysolda shook her head, though he couldn't see her. Hari, at last swept up in the man's words, said a hoarse, 'No.'

'Then I should have started further back—'

Aunty cleared her throat pointedly and Uncle hurried on. 'But I will press on. Most realms have their stories about these lines that cross the earth. Connect it. That along these channels are places where gifted people are found in abundance, where the crops are bountiful and the mines generous.'

Ysolda thought of the map on the Hull Hall's wall, the

silver stitches linking Glaw Wood to the Lakes and on to Norveger. Were the lines what they depicted?

'There are many products of these lines. The Anchorite is one of its wonders, the Sea Henge a second, the Drakken Peaks a third, the Hell Gate another.'

Ysolda couldn't stop herself. She choked out a short laugh, trying to turn it into a cough. Uncle sank into offended silence and Ysolda pulled an apologetic face before remembering the absolute darkness. 'Sorry, Uncle. But, the Hell Gate? Surely you do not believe—'

'That when we are dead, our souls live on? That there are halls of the dead? Yes, I do.'

There was little Ysolda could say to that. She bit her tongue, and Uncle took up his telling again, with a tone of superiority. 'But these places of plenty are also places of danger. Through them runs the spirit of the earth, and that is a powerful thing. It allows the world to speak across its million miles, and if needed, to restore balance. Those who were watching the wolf queen's progress realised she was focusing her efforts on places where these lines intersected – where their power is most potent. Sometimes they are marked with henges – stone circles to concentrate their influence. They overlaid the map of her conquests with the maps of the ley lines – an exact match. It is then they started to speak of the Geomancer.'

Uncle paused for effect, and a ripple spread through the

prisoners. Ysolda's voice was barely a whisper as she repeated the word. 'Geomancer.'

It tasted dangerous.

'Yes. This is the crux of it all, her ultimate goal.' Uncle's words threw Ysolda back to Glaw Wood, when she stood before the wolf queen's runaway daughter and the girl had used that exact phrase – *her ultimate goal*. The thing the Anchorite was a stepping stone towards. The Geomancer.

'What is it?'

'What are they, you mean. The Geomancer is a person in whom all these powers can reside. A vessel for the spirit of the world. Someone who can control the entirety of the earth-magic.'

'It's impossible, of course,' sighed Aunty. 'We don't even know what form it would take—'

'The Anchorite does,' said Uncle. 'That is why Seren needs to find her.'

'But even if the queen could become the Geomancer, it would hollow her out. Destroy her. No one person is meant to hold all that power,' replied Aunty.

'You think that will stop her trying? See already what her attempts have caused,' said Uncle. 'Quakes, tidal waves, forest fires. And she is not the only one. Thane Boreal seeks the power too.'

Ysolda thought of the Rhyg, created by one quake and

deepened by a second when they came for Hari. Of Glaw Wood, bereft of birdsong.

'It will worsen now, if she fails.'

'Wait,' said Hari. 'If she *fails*? Surely you don't want her to succeed in this quest, Uncle?'

'It is worse for the world, of course,' he said slowly. 'But best for us. The world is turning away from us. Turning on us. It would be better, and worse, if the queen does not fail.

'Let me explain. We humans have lived in harmony with the world for many centuries. How many centuries, there is some argument, though far enough back for the Anchorite to be truly ancient. But we are tipping the balance now. Using more wood than the trees can grow, eating more fish than the sea has to give. We are part of nature, yes, but we have also set ourselves against it.'

'Maybe where you're from,' said Hari hotly. 'But in Glaw Wood, we take only—'

'What you need?' Uncle chuckled again. 'Child, we all take what we need. But what we need becomes more and more. And then what? What about what the world needs? What if that is exactly counter to our existence? What if Thane Boreal, famously bloodthirsty, succeeds? The wolf queen may be a monster, but she is our monster. We need her to triumph.'

Ysolda's ears were ringing. She barely heard Hari's

next questions. 'So what now? What happens when she finds the Anchorite?'

'She gets the answers she needs, the knowledge of how to become the Geomancer.'

'But why did she take Hari?' said Ysolda. 'She could have asked anyone in Glaw Wood where the End-World Wood was.'

'She has not only taken Hari, has she? She has imprisoned all of us, for protection against rivals to her quest. Only a gifted person could challenge her now.'

'But who would want that?' said Ysolda. 'To be the Geomancer?' It sounded awful, terrifying and ridiculous.

'Thane Boreal, for one. Her daughter, for another,' said Aunty.

Ysolda turned her head to the woman's voice, saying, 'Eira?' at the same time as Hari said, 'She has a daughter?'

'You know her name,' said the woman.

'I met her, in Glaw Wood.'

Ysolda felt Hari's flinch of surprise. The woman's voice hid a smile. 'What did you think of her?'

'Not much.'

Aunty laughed. 'She is not the easiest. She has her mother's ferocity. Not to be underestimated. I was her nurse.'

'Really?' Ysolda wrinkled her nose. She couldn't imagine this kind-voiced woman helping create such a beast.

'She even called me Amma. She was born here, a child of

the Lakes. But she seeks the power of all her mother possesses.' Aunty paused. 'They don't get along.'

'But she's a child?' asked Hari. 'So she cannot think to succeed?'

'No one can, without the Anchorite. At least she doesn't know where the End-World Wood is.'

Tingles of dread spread through Ysolda's fingers. She cleared her throat. 'She does know. I told her. Well, showed her. On a map.'

There was a moment's pause.

The woman sucked in her breath, teeth rattling. 'That,' she said seriously, 'may be a problem.'

CHAPTER EIGHTEEN

PART

Ysolda must have slept, for she dreamed. She was on a boat, big as the Hull Hall, alone. The water was smooth and endless, endless. Red as blood, as the sky on the road to the castle. A light grew at the horizon, like a rising sun, but with the same underwater quality as the light lining the castle walls. It was so bright it burned her eyes, burned her vision into blackness.

She woke with a chill in her veins, Hari's arms wrapped tight around her, their foreheads pressed against each other. Her sister was cool as stone, and Ysolda held her breath to check she could feel Hari's. It hit her cheek, reassuringly warm.

'Are you staring at me?' Hari's voice was thick with sleep.

'Your breath stinks.'

A low laugh. 'No wild mint here. No birch twigs to scrub.' Sadness crept into her tone. Ysolda wished she could see her sister's face. She could imagine it well enough, the worry line pinched between her brows, eyes anxious. Ysolda longed to go back to sleep, for the discomfort of waking on hard, damp rock to vanish, for the possibility of light to be only an eyelid away.

'I still can't believe you're here,' said Hari. 'I was so worried you'd been hurt in the quake, but I never imagined they'd take you too.'

There was so much she hadn't told Hari. About Eira and the amulet, about the Rhyg swallowing their house and her journey through the forest, about Deepti and Sami and the red storm – but right now she didn't want to talk about any of that. Nor about the journey that lay ahead, all the fears she had. She wanted only to talk about home. 'I left Sorrell with Fyona,' she said. 'She was grumpy, but fine.'

'She's always grumpy,' said Hari, and there was relief in her voice. 'But I'm glad she's all right. She ran off when the Ryders broke down the door. Where is Nara?'

'Waiting, outside.'

'I miss her. I miss the trees. Since being down here I've realised how much I even miss their endless chatter. But at least they put me in here with others. When I first arrived it was only me in a tiny room of rock, barely big enough to stand in. I felt like the Anchorite in her chamber.'

'But she's not real,' said Ysolda. 'Is she?'

'Of course not,' said Hari. 'I only mean it was small.'

'Why did they keep you in there?'

'The amulet,' said Hari solemnly, and Ysolda pressed her lips together. 'They thought I had it, was keeping it secret from them. They wanted it badly.'

'Why?'

'The queen needs it. But at least the amulet is safe at home. We would be even more lost without it.'

Ysolda's hands bunched as the impulse to lie swept over her. She fiddled with the buckle of her boot and her palm brushed the obsidian, the blade so sharp she did not immediately realise she'd cut herself. Then it began to sting. 'Roots!'

'What happened?'

'I cut myself.' It was the exact place where Ani's spear had pierced, the skin already thin and sore. She felt Hari's hands search for hers.

'Do you have moss?'

'Somewhere.' She searched her pockets and gave it to her sister, who tore out the uppermost tendrils to get at the clean layer beneath and pressed it to her palm. The moss began its healing work instantly, but without willow bark to soothe, it stung nearly as badly as the cut itself. Ysolda tried to draw away, but Hari held tightly.

In a rush, she said, 'Sometimes the cure is as bad as the cut. You must be careful. Trust nothing she says. Trust only yourself, only Nara. Remember who you are, where you came from. What you are part of.'

Ysolda heard a tearing sound as Hari ripped off a piece of cloth from her tunic and tied it around Ysolda's palm, holding the moss in place. An awful realisation was seeping in even as the pain ebbed away. She would have to tell the truth.

'Hari,' she said again, and her sister waited patiently in the dark quiet. 'Your amulet.'

'I don't mind that you took it,' said Hari. 'But it's safe at home now?'

How could Ysolda tell her she had let a stranger steal it? But, though the plan was built of ash, easily blown apart, she knew where the girl was headed. She would help the queen get to the End-World Wood, and retrieve the amulet from her daughter.

'Yes,' she lied, grateful for the darkness, hands balling, cut palm stinging. She would fix this, and turn her lie to truth. 'At home.'

Hari's grip relaxed. 'When we are home, together, I'll tell you about it. The amulet. It's not just for listening, you know.'

'I know,' said Ysolda. 'You told me the story about the Anchorite tapping it from the Elder Alder—'

'No, not a story. It's a piece of history – of deep time. It matters more than you can know.'

This did not make Ysolda feel better.

The sisters let their hands rest over each other's a moment, breathing together.

'Do you think it's true, what Uncle said?'

'Which part?' Hari's voice was wary.

'All of it, any of it.'

'There are probably seeds of truth. That the wolf queen has many names, that there are thin places, where the world's layers rub like cloth and fray into one another. We know this, don't we? We see it in the forest, all the time. Owls roost in one tree, wake in another. Dead trees feed new ones through hidden weavings. It's a circle, one we are part of. All connected.'

'And the Anchorite?'

'No,' said Hari, definitely. 'A tree can live a thousand years, but a girl? Not in one form, in one body. Such things are beyond humans, as they should be.'

'But the wolf queen believes it's true—'

'Because she wants it to be. Because she wants power, as Uncle said.'

Ysolda was aware of the old man's snores, not so far off. She lowered her voice even more. 'He seemed to say it would be better if she succeeded.'

'She can't succeed, because such power does not exist.'

'And the halls of the dead?'

Hari's breath hitched. 'I know such thoughts are comforting. That it does not end. But we don't believe that and still, we go on, don't we? In our stories, our bloodlines, our ashes on the wind.'

Ysolda tried to push the tears down, but they filled her eyes and her throat, spilled down her cheeks. 'What if I can't find the wood? What if the queen gets angry when she finds there is no Anchorite?'

Hari pulled her to her chest. Ysolda could feel her heart beating. Her big sister was silent because she didn't have the answers, and among her fear Ysolda felt an odd sort of pride that Hari was treating her as a grown-up, someone who could know there was not an easy answer, or even an answer at all.

'It will be all right. I love you.'

Uncle's snores stopped abruptly, and Ysolda heard him yawn. 'Have they come for the girl yet?'

'I'm still here.'

'Give me your hand.'

Ysolda held out her palm, the moss-covered cut aching as Uncle held her hand in his warm, dry one. His skin was very soft, loose over his knuckles.

'You are hurt?' he said.

'A small cut.'

'The Forgiver demands blood, so at least you can shed it easily.'

Ysolda tried to withdraw, but he held on.

'Do not be afraid of her. The Forgiver. She was a girl, once, too. Remember that, about all of them. They are people, and no better than you. Even Raani, Seren, no matter how many names she collects.'

'Thank you, Uncle.'

'Blessings on you, child. I hope she sees your safe return.'

'Sees it?' said Hari.

'All will be clear. None of what I have told you is to scare you. Only to prepare you. It is better to walk with your eyes open, yes?'

'Yes, Uncle.'

Uncle patted Ysolda on the top of her head. She found the warm weight of it comforting. 'My daughter was like you. She believed she lived in a different world from me, that the things I told her weren't true. But truth works only one way. It stays intact however you look at it.'

'Uncle,' said Aunty softly. 'Let her be with her sister. They'll come soon.'

And so they did. The noise of the key filled the chamber, and the light rushed in like it had in Ysolda's dream: blinding, powerful, like a wave. She blinked as fast as she could, eyes streaming, desperate to catch a glimpse of Hari before the general took her. The prisoners gathered at the back of the cave, Hari holding Ysolda tight.

'Come, child,' said the general, backed by the slicing glare of two Ryders, Ani and Cai, already striding forward to take her.

'Be brave,' said Hari into her ear, and as Ysolda was pulled away she finally was able to look at her sister's face, at her acorn-brown eyes, and pale skin, and clever hands, and the crease between her brows. Around her were clustered the other prisoners: she saw a man who must be Uncle, back ramrod straight, staring at her with misty eyes. Aunty had a long braid threaded with grey, and pockmarks pitting her face from her cheek to her neck. They had their arms around Hari, who was trembling.

'I will see you again,' said Ysolda. 'I love you.'

If Hari answered, Ysolda did not hear it. The door closed, the key turned, and though the Ryders steered her towards the stairs, towards daylight, Ysolda felt as though it was she who had been left behind in a brutal dark.

CHAPTER NINETEEN

THE FORGIVER

The general was glancing sideways at Ysolda but pretending not to, and Ysolda was pretending not to notice, focusing on stopping the tears sliding down her cheeks with the sleeves of her tunic. Beside the tall, well-groomed woman, she felt suddenly very dirty, her clothes smelly from days of walking and sleeping in them, her skin grimy and her fingernails black.

She had never noticed the small ways Hari took care of her, like washing her hands and feet in water from the spring each day, or fraying birch twigs each week to use as brushes for their teeth and tongues, but without them she felt like she was coming apart at the seams. *Remember who you are.*

She stemmed her tears as they reached the top of the

steps. As soon as they broke out into dawn, Ysolda looked for Nara. There were no birds swirling overhead, and the castle blocked her view of the beach. As she searched, a wolf stared down over the edge. Its face was calm, but as it yawned Ysolda saw its teeth were sharp as the blade stored safely in her boot. Her palm throbbed.

The general spoke not a word to her. They walked, not to the Hull Hall nor the larger entrance chamber, but around the outside of the castle, the curve of the upturned ships dizzying.

'This way,' said Ani.

Finally they reached the beach, a mix of fine sand and rounded pebbles that clattered and slid beneath Ysolda's feet. A line of dunes lay ahead, hiding the sea, and to the left of the castle was a low ridge of rock into which were set the dark mouths of caves. Perhaps the caves were part of the same network in which Hari and the others were imprisoned. They seemed made of the same kind of rock, but open to the elements were carved by rain and wind as well as sea, curved and gnarled like old roots.

Not all the caves were dark. One stood orange and glowing, like an amber bead set among onyx. Ysolda remembered the amulet, the thief, and her face flushed with anger. Before the lit cave were four wolves and the unmistakable outline of a woman on wolfback. Seren was waiting.

The queen, though tiny in comparison to her wolf, still possessed an enormous presence. Her hair was tightly braided, hanging in a thick black rope over her sky-blue tunic, long enough to reach her knees and matched to deep blue leggings and a shawl of brilliant copper weave across her shoulders. Ysolda had never seen such deep pigment, the thread made from metal thin enough to bend like fabric. Around her neck was a thick torc of gold, a beaten semicircle of brilliance – the sun made metal. She looked otherworldly, and Ysolda remembered Uncle's words: *They are people, and no better than you. Even Raani, Seren.*

Beside the queen and the wolves was a sullen-faced and familiar figure – Sami, neck strewn with fool's gold, loaded like a mule with packs and flasks. He held the reins of the other wolves in his hands, and as they approached Ysolda tried to catch his eye, but he only scowled harder.

Ysolda looked for Nara everywhere, but before she could sight her hawk the general nudged her towards where the queen waited before the mouth of the lit cave.

Seren dismounted. 'Forgiver?' she called into the cave. 'Are you ready?'

Ysolda heard no response, but the wind was high on the exposed beach and Seren seemed to have received an answer, for she beckoned her and the Ryders forward.

Ysolda was pulled unwillingly to the entrance, Sami following, and peered inside.

It was a different world. On the walls stretched paintings in red and white, handprints and trees, long scratches gouged in spirals and symbols, all illuminated by a fire at the centre of the space, stacked expertly and scented with an unfamiliar perfume, heavy and sweet as smoked honey. At the back, a tunnel stretched into the dark like a gullet, cold air sucking.

The Ryders forced Ysolda inside, positioning her beside the general. Sami was placed between Ani and Cai, and the queen stood before the tunnel, firelight bouncing off her shining hair, showing the copper and blue tones of it, making the metal threads of the shawl dance. The only sounds were the crackling of the fire, the faint calls of the gulls on the beach outside.

Ysolda glanced around at the walls. She recognised the Ogham for *stop*, the leaf shapes of oak and poplar, fish and wolves drawn in a mixture of paint and engraving. In the flames the illustrated walls stretched and contracted like a ribcage, the animals breathed, the trees swayed. It made Ysolda dizzy and she looked away, blinking through the fire at the queen's back.

Beyond Seren came movement. A figure emerging from the tunnel. The glinting of many teeth, something pointed rising from a pale face. Ysolda wanted to move away, but she was pinned to the spot by the general on one side, Ani on the other. The queen moved aside, and the Forgiver stepped into the firelight.

She wore antlers bound to her head like a twisted crown, the deer's skull split and wrapped over her cheeks so its teeth lined her cheekbones. There were more teeth slung on necklaces around her neck, and the antlers were tipped with gold. In the flickering light they glittered like the queen's torc, like blades and a shield held up ready for battle.

Beneath the skull headdress Ysolda saw a face far younger than she had expected – a girl Hari's age, skin unlined and pale as though the sun had never touched her. Her blue eyes were almost clear in the firelight, her hair a white cloud cut close to her head to better fit the skull of the deer. She was robed in furs and her build was slight. Her eyes slid around the cave, over the Ryders and the queen, over Ysolda. A crease appeared between her brows, a clarity coming into her gaze for a moment, before the queen cleared her throat. 'In your own time, Forgiver.'

The Forgiver raised her arms. Something stitched into the lining of her furs rattled, like seeds in a poppyhead, and she started to sway from side to side, chanting. Her shadow stretched on to the cave wall. Ysolda didn't recognise the words, but her skin prickled in response to the sound. It felt sacred somehow, magic and ancient.

Beautiful. The queen closed her eyes and swayed too, in time with the Forgiver.

Still chanting, the girl kicked up dust from the cave floor into the fire. It reacted with the flames, sparking and emitting sharp puffs and popping sounds. Ani stepped back, swearing under her breath, but at a glare from the general she moved into place again.

The Forgiver walked around the fire in a circle, passing close to the flames so her furs singed and smoked. She held something in her outstretched hands, and nodded first at the queen. Seren pressed her palm on to one of the antlers, hissing as she did so, and held it over whatever the Forgiver had in her hands.

The Forgiver moved to the general, who also cut her palm on the antler, and Ysolda saw the oracle held six stones, one for each of them assembled in the cave. They had obviously been collected from the beach, worn smooth by the sea and various shades of pale grey and purple, some striped with bands of quartz and engraved with unfamiliar runes. All of them had holes through their centres. In Glaw Wood they called them hag stones, and there were superstitions around looking through them and seeing portals to another world.

Blood shimmered on two of the stones, and now the Forgiver stood before Ysolda, her pale blue eyes meeting hers. The chanting reverberated through Ysolda, buzzing in her chest. The Forgiver bent her head, and Ysolda followed her gaze down, thinking she was looking at something unpleasant on her tunic. But the general nudged her. 'Your hand,' she hissed.

Understanding, Ysolda removed the moss wadding and pressed her palm to the antler tip. It was serrated, and the wound reopened easily. Beads of blood sprang up and Ysolda hastily held her hand over the stones. She was not fast enough, and the blood dropped on to one of the already smeared pebbles before she could anoint a clean one. The Forgiver's eyes flicked back to Ysolda's. As it had before, her gaze snapped into sharper focus and she gave a wink, so quick Ysolda could have imagined it.

The general had not noticed the wink, and as the Forgiver moved on to the Ryders and Sami, she leaned in and explained. 'The stone is our resolution, solid and unyielding. The blood represents a sacrifice, penance for the blood we may shed of others.'

Ysolda gulped.

When all of them had bled on the stones, the Forgiver turned with a burst of energy and threw them on to the fire. The flames sprung up as the stones hit the logs, and Ysolda gasped as they flashed suddenly green and gold. Sami too stepped back, but he was shunted into the circle by Cai.

'Fire, to forge the sacrifice and meld it with our resolution, make firm our will and our apology,' said the general dispassionately. The Ryders and the queen were still, clearly used to this process, this ritual, but there was a furious intensity, almost fear in the queen's face as her eyes latched not on to the fire, but the Forgiver.

The girl's antlered head was bowed, and she was chanting more quietly now, staring at and leaning so close to the fire the fur of the skinned animal she wore smoked. But the girl did not move away, not until the flames stopped singing green and gold and became normal tongues of red and yellow. Then she reached into the fire and pulled the rocks from the heat. Ysolda winced as she heard the hiss of flesh from the boiling hot stones imprinting on the Forgiver's palm, but the girl didn't so much as flinch.

'Now?' Ysolda murmured.

'Now, she reads them.'

The Forgiver had stopped chanting and was studying the rocks carefully. Ysolda saw they had turned iridescent in the heat, like raven's wings in sunlight, black rainbows glinting on their surfaces. What did the Forgiver see? Did she know Ysolda had her own quest, her own reasons for finding the End-World Wood and the thief that had her amulet?

The Forgiver examined the rocks one by one, blew a quick breath on them and placed them down on a flat rock before her. But when she reached the fourth rock, she frowned.

The queen, who had not broken her fierce attention on the girl, spoke immediately. 'What is it? What do you see?'

The Forgiver looked up, not at the queen, but at Ysolda. 'You,' she said, in an unfamiliar accent. 'Come.'

'The girl?' said the queen. 'What do you see for her? Tell me!'

The Forgiver ignored her, moving around the fire towards Ysolda. Her pale-eyed gaze was fixed, and she was pointing outside, out to the dunes and the grey sea beyond.

'Forgiver?' prompted Seren. She made to step out of the circle and follow the girl, but the Forgiver shook her head.

'Stay.'

Ysolda couldn't imagine anyone telling the queen what to do, but Seren accepted it.

'Go,' she snapped, almost resentfully. 'Quickly.'

The Forgiver was at the cave mouth now, and Ysolda looked uncertainly up at the general, who glared. 'You heard the queen. Go.'

CHAPTER TWENTY

KORE

Ysolda tripped after the Forgiver, eyes blinded by the flat pinkish light of sunrise, full of sparks from the fire. Even in her furs, the girl looked insubstantial in this glare, like a spirit moving across the pebble beach and on to the dunes, her cloak erasing her footsteps from the soft sand and leaving a smooth passage that Ysolda followed, shuddering as she passed the wolf.

They crested the dunes, the sharp grasses spiking Ysolda's ankles, and the sea spread before them, choppy and opaque, gulls bobbing like small boats across its expanse. Ysolda scanned the brightening sky, and with an enormous surge of relief saw Nara wheeling overhead. The hawk saw her, too, but Ysolda shook her head, gesturing with her palm to keep the hawk away.

The Forgiver stopped at the sea edge, the retreating tide leaving licks of scum across the damp sand. Seaweed bloomed in red and green knots, shells and pebbles shining on the shore. The Forgiver turned to Ysolda, and her face was transformed. Gone was the careful blankness; the calm and smooth of her features turned spiky and alive. It was like watching someone move from sleep to wakefulness in an instant.

She pulled off her antler headdress. Her hair was wispy beneath, plastered to her skull. 'Ugh,' she said, scratching her scalp. 'That's better.'

Ysolda gaped at her, and she grinned.

'Who are you then? Another oracle?'

Ysolda checked the dune, but the girl didn't look around. 'No one will come. I told them to stay.'

'Why does she do what you say?'

'She believes us oracles powerful. She collects us,' said the Forgiver, 'but I'm the best. Even in Delphi, I was the ruler's favourite. I'm Kore, by the way.'

Ysolda's head was spinning. 'Ysolda. I'm not an oracle.'

'Oh.' The girl wrinkled her nose. 'Why are you here then? You're not from the Lakes.'

'I have to lead her to the End-World Wood. She's looking for the Anchorite.'

'And Eira, surely?'

'Do you know her?'

'Of course.' There was something unreadable in Kore's voice.

'She's a thief. She took – something from me.'

Kore laughed softly. 'She takes something from everyone. She's a magpie, a borrower, a collector of things. Like her mother. What did she take from you?'

Ysolda hesitated. She didn't know whether to fully trust Kore or not. 'A necklace.'

'I see.' Ysolda was worried she really did, as Kore gazed at her. 'So you're a navigator?'

'I'm just . . . me.'

'I wouldn't let Seren know that,' said Kore. 'She likes to believe people are special. She thinks she is, so she surrounds herself with the best. Like Shiv.'

'Shiv?'

'Shivani. The general. She's the best warrior in the world. I'm the best oracle. So you should at least pretend to be the best navigator.'

Ysolda's head was spinning. The way the Forgiver had switched from impressive, slightly scary oracle to normal, albeit very pale girl, was dizzying. She was worried it was a trick. 'I don't understand. Why are you talking to me like this?'

'Because I thought you were like me. You are, sort of. She's collected you, too.' Kore started to straighten her headdress. 'But if you don't want to talk—'

'You didn't see something? In my stone?'

'Oh, I did,' said Kore. 'That's why I thought you were special. That stone says you'll need to be.'

'What,' said Ysolda, trying not to feel silly about asking after a speaking stone, 'did it say?'

In a monotone, Kore intoned, 'You're going on a journey. Not the one you think you're on. You'll need to root into the wound. You'll lose the one you love three times. You'll see the clouds as a sea. You'll see roots as constellations. In the highest place you'll find the deepest time. In the deepest place you'll find the brightest light. You're on a path to all that now. There's no stopping it.'

Ysolda blinked stupidly. *Roots? Wounds? Constellations?* She felt she was back in the castle, listening to a language she didn't understand, random words reaching her through the babble. 'A path to what?'

Kore shrugged. 'I suppose that depends which route you take.'

Ysolda felt her impatience rising. 'That doesn't mean anything.'

'Maybe not at the moment. But it will soon enough.'

'And that's real, is it? Because all this –' Ysolda waved her hand at the cloak, the antler headdress – 'seems like an act.'

'It is,' said Kore, unconcerned. 'The antlers were a Delphi thing, but it stuck. I coat the stones in ore dust so the fire changes colour. It doesn't only matter what I say, it also matters how I say it. The queen loves stories – you should remember that. Tell her the right one in the right way, and she will trust you, or even better, fear you. Because I look like this –' Kore gestured at her pale skin and hair – 'she both fears and trusts me. Because she saw me have an attack in Delphi, she believes me above all others.'

'An attack?'

'I have fits. I black out, shake, sometimes swallow my tongue.'

Ysolda remembered Ani and the general speaking about the Forgiver's attacks after she lied about the End-World Wood. 'That sounds awful.'

'It's rough,' shuddered Kore, 'but it feeds her vision of me. It's what's kept me safe. Because I have fits, because I was born without colour in my skin, she thinks I am unique. It protects me here as it did in Delphi.'

'Protects you from what?'

Kore looked at her quizzically. 'From my difference being seen as bad. People don't like people who are not like them. Surely you know that.'

Ysolda thought of how she'd first felt when she saw the Ryders, and then the Forgiver herself. Not only fearful, but suspicious because she'd never seen their like before. Now she felt guilty about it, but what Kore was saying made sense.

'What do I do?' said Ysolda. 'What the stone said, about losing the one I love – that must be my sister.'

Kore shrugged. 'This doesn't work like that. There aren't names, places, times or dates. I work from instinct, impressions. I can't tell you more than I know. But I can give you this.'

She held out her hand, in which was one of the hag stones, the one Ysolda had bled on. The fire had transformed it into a scorched sequence of cracks, splintering out like stars. Ysolda saw Kore's palm beneath it was thick with scars: burns from the stones. So she did feel pain. That too was part of the act.

'Make an amulet of it,' said the Forgiver. 'Here, use this.'

She ripped one of the fine hide tassels from her headdress and looped it through the hole, creating a necklace. Ysolda bent her neck and the Forgiver tied it around her throat.

'What will this do?'

'A lot of this is for show, for a good story,' said Kore, gesturing at herself, her headdress. 'To make the queen feel better about the slaughter that is necessary to keep her power, the cruelty that advances it. But I am real,' she said, a flash of ferocity in her voice. 'And what I saw in this stone is real too. It's a reading of your future. You should keep it with you. Show the Anchorite, if you find her. And before that, it will help you see more clearly.'

'How do you mean?'

'Look through it on foggy days. It will clear the mists.'

This made as little sense as anything else, but Ysolda was hungry for answers. 'What will the queen do with the Anchorite, if we do find her?' she whispered, forgetting she didn't believe the ancient girl existed.

'Nothing good. But perhaps it is the lesser of a greater evil,' the Forgiver said, unknowingly echoing Uncle. 'Or at least, a greater threat.'

'The Geomancer?'

Kore looked at her sharply. 'I thought you said you were just a navigator?'

'I'm not even that. Someone told me the story.'

'Story,' said Kore thoughtfully. 'Maybe. We should get back.'

'Wait.' Ysolda whistled, and Nara came at once, landing heavily on her shoulder. Ysolda bent her forehead to the soft feathers of Nara's belly, and the bird pulled her hair affectionately. 'Nara,' she breathed. 'I missed you.'

'Yours?' said Kore.

'We go together,' said Ysolda. 'You must stay at a distance, all right? We'll be on the wolves, so follow them.'

Nara gave a purr of acknowledgement and took off again, worrying the gulls into flight. The girls watched the white panic of them bloom over the sea as Nara swooped, enjoying their fear.

Ysolda felt like the grey sky was pressing down on her.

The bad night's sleep in the damp cave had made her bones chilled and leaden. The memory of Hari's warmth made her want to cry. 'I don't want to go. Can't you get me out of it? Say – I don't know – anything.'

'No,' said Kore, pulling on her headdress. 'You're going. I'm sorry, but that much is clear.' With the headdress on she looked again fearsome and otherworldly.

Ysolda straightened her back in response. If Kore could place another face over her own, maybe she could too. A navigator. A storyteller. Yes. She could be that.

'But remember what I've told you. And take courage,' the Forgiver said, walking up the dune. 'Maybe you'll turn out to be special after all.'

CHAPTER TWENTY-ONE

PACK

Wolves moved nothing like horses. They weaved and slunk, anticipating rather than responding to commands, and when they broke into a run their pace was such that Ysolda closed her eyes in fear. She clutched the general's waist, whose red cloak whipped around Ysolda's face as the wolves left the beach and the castle of broken boats behind and entered the green heart of the Lakes.

As Kore had said, the Ryders and their queen had stayed in the cave just as they were ordered, while the Forgiver had turned from oracle to girl and back again. Though Seren's curiosity was clear, she accepted Kore's proclamation of satisfaction silently, and when Kore said they were forgiven a look of great peace washed over her features.

Ysolda felt sure they would know what had passed

between them, but Kore's act was strong and no one noticed the hag stone hung around her neck, concealed beneath her tunic. The other hag stones were returned to the fire, presumably to await the next ritual. Ysolda wondered what Kore had seen in the others' futures.

Kore's prophecy rang in Ysolda's ears. *You'll see the clouds as a sea. You'll see roots as constellations.* And most of all, *You'll lose the one you love three times.* Ysolda shuddered and the general grunted, elbowing her arms looser.

Ysolda dared to open her eyes a crack. Green blurred past. The hillsides here were uneven, pitted with burrows and anthills, yellow gorse just starting to pattern its sides like patches of sunshine. That surely was not right – flowers just blooming at the end of summer? Ysolda thought of the map Eira had drawn in the dirt, how little of the ground they had covered from Glaw Wood to the castle – how much remained before they reached the End-World Wood.

Her deception had already begun. Ysolda knew that the last remnants of the mythical wood lay on a tidal island at the most north-easterly point of the land, but until she had seen Eira's make-do map she'd had no concept of how far that was. Her navigation was limited to the sun's rise and fall, the North Star's anchorage in the night sky – she never needed more in Glaw Wood, whose hollows and rises she knew like her sister's face.

But the Forgiver had told her the queen needed stories, and this was one thing Ysolda could do. Stories were how they kept their history, made sense of weather and death, and if Ysolda needed to tell some to keep the queen happy, she would.

Before they mounted the wolves, Seren turned to Ysolda.

'The Forgiver has told me not to question you and I will not. She has earned my trust over many years, but you are as unknown to me as the bottom of the sea. Steer us false and you will pay, understand? This is not a quest with base stakes – all the world will fall if you disobey me.'

Ysolda had summoned some of Kore's pale-eyed mystery to herself. 'I understand, Queen. We will take the most direct route.' She'd pointed north-east. 'Ride until we meet the sea, and then north until it sits at our two sides. There is the tree, and the Anchorite.'

'You are certain?' There had been hunger in her voice once more.

'Yes, my queen.'

Oh no oh no oh no, beat her heart. The general glanced at her suspiciously. Ysolda decided to pull back the mystical tone a little.

Nara swooped in and out of view, obvious to Ysolda as a red star in the birdless sky, but no one else was looking up. Everyone was intent on the landscape ahead, the green, treeless roll of the hills.

The Lakes lived up to their name. Every dip held a pool of water at its base, encircled by hills that toothed jaggedly into the grey sky. The wolves were undaunted by the peaks, running easily, the sweat shedding from their flanks.

It quickly became clear the queen was not going to stop for anything so mundane as food. They ate on wolfback, the general directing Ysolda to search through the packs strapped to the beast's side. There was a sort of lace-thin flatbread, wrapped so well it was still billowing steam when she broke it to share, and a fried cake made of green beans. It was unfamiliar food, and Ysolda wondered whether it was from the queen's homeland or one of her realms. Either way, it tasted good, like mint and something spicy she had no name for. She must have made an appreciative sound because the general said, 'Dosa and peas puri – better than your Glaw Wood muck, isn't it?'

Ysolda bristled, but she couldn't argue. This was no bread and hard cheese. 'Dosa?'

'Bread, made with rice flour.'

'Riss?'

'Rice.' The general laughed. Being on the road and eating the food had obviously lifted her mood. 'We eat it all the time at home, in the south. We brought a seed store with us, collected crops from each of the realms. If there's one thing these isles have going for them, it's rain. Good for growing. Good for rice.'

'Rice,' repeated Ysolda. 'And this? Peas?'

'A green bean of a sort, sweet and spiced with mint and cumin. The cooks keep a spice cupboard, and anyone can trade for them. The queen is generous with her supplies.'

Ysolda considered this as she chewed. There were servants at the castle, and the castle itself was a reminder of the queen's brutality – all those broken boats – but she clearly inspired loyalty too. And she had good taste in food. It filled Ysolda's belly warmly and, used to the rhythm of the wolf by now, she was able to doze with her arms still hooked tight around the general. She thought of Kore and Eira – these strange, maddening girls that surrounded the queen – who was herself the most strange.

There were other courts of women, but never, in Ysolda's limited knowledge, one so successful as Seren's. In the stories of the wolf queen told around flickering fires, Gwyn making shapes of his hands and throwing shadows across the surrounding trunks to make wolves and boats and swords, there was always one line repeated – *and so her reach grew, until there was no day's end to her realms*. Had Ysolda ever imagined she would be here, beside her, eating food grown from seeds brought from one end of her domain to the other?

Ysolda's eyes closed deeper, the rocking of the wolf almost lulling.

*

She woke to early morning. Overhead the sky stretched purple, stitched with fading stars, the dust of the constellations dulled by the arriving sun. Ysolda was hungry again, and her hands were numb with cold around the general's middle. She realised what had woken her – they had stopped, and the general was now unlatching Ysolda's fingers. Ysolda shoved them beneath her armpits to keep warm as the general dismounted.

From her vantage point Ysolda looked drowsily around. They were beside a lake, on a beach of pebbles. She had no idea how far they had ridden, but in case the queen was watching she nodded knowingly to herself, like she knew exactly where they were. Still in the Lakes, that much was obvious, but the landscape had changed from rolling green to grey. The hills were formed of scree, loose rocks still tumbling from the wolves' descent to the pebble beach. Ysolda's stomach swooped as she imagined the larger boulders near the peak tumbling down and crushing their makeshift camp.

Sami met her eyes blearily. He had clearly slept too – the metal clasp of Cai's cloak was imprinted in his cheek.

'Until mid-morning,' the queen was saying. Ani was hurriedly laying rolled pieces of fabric on to the stones. She untied each one and unfurled it into a human-length padded mat, thin but enough to protect from the toothy pebbles. 'Just so the wolves can rest a while. Eat, and you two, start a fire, fill the water.'

She was gesturing at Ysolda and Sami, but all her attention was on her wolf. Seren rode with the fewest trappings of all, using only a set of leather reins and a pack strapped to her wolf's ruff. She removed them now and smoothed the wolf's fur where it had rubbed. 'There, Tej. Is that better?'

She rested her forehead against its muzzle, a woman and her wolf silhouetted by water. The wolf bounded into the lake, splashing Seren's fine clothes, but she only laughed. It began to swim and chomp at the water, and Ysolda realised it was fishing. A silver flash quickly muddied the water red. Once unsaddled, the other three wolves joined in its hunt, the queen watching, hands on hips. But when she turned to their makeshift camp, her eyes were cool and hard once more.

'Fire,' she snapped at Ysolda. 'Quickly.'

She settled cross-legged on one of the mats, and Ani brought her more dosa and peas puri. Ysolda started scanning the ground while Sami searched the hillside, pulling up bracken and roots. Nara settled atop the hill, and Ysolda wished she had an excuse to go and sit with her, to stroke her soft feathers.

She went towards Sami instead, glad of the chance to speak more with the boy. He had a good bundle already, and he scowled at her when she came to join him.

'I've got this,' he said. 'You find a flint, make a firepit.'

Stung, Ysolda went back to the circle of mats. The Ryders were sitting one to each, and it was clear the last, raggedy cloth was for her and Sami to share. Keeping her head down, she moved into the ring and stacked pebbles in a circle to create a barrier from the breeze, taking rocks from the centre to allow the fire to sit deep under it. When no one was looking she pulled the flint from her tunic.

Sami brought the kindling and roots and Ysolda set to striking it into flame, thinking of the obsidian in her boot, the hag stone around her neck, the flint in her palm. Her world had been all wood, and now she was surrounded by stone.

CHAPTER TWENTY-TWO

REST

When the fire was burning strongly, Ani and Cai shouldered Ysolda and Sami aside and set a metal kettle in the flames, a couple of the fish fetched by the wolves put atop flat stones. Ysolda had never seen a kettle before, shiny and burnished by fire, the workmanship so fine there were even engravings on the lid. To it Ani added some dried berries and leaves.

The wolves had finished fishing and were drying themselves on the bank, curled around one another like a massive pile of rugs. The queen had called them each by name to the bank – hers was Tej, Ani's was Bala, Cai's Haddi, and the one Ysolda and the general rode was Ravi. The scale of them was still unnerving to Ysolda, but she was feeling more kindly towards them, seeing how they played and lay together like a pack of dogs. She thought to share this with Sami, but his face was closed as ever.

When the tea and fish were cooked, Ysolda was amazed that she and Sami were given the same as the queen and the Ryders. Seren was fed first of course, but then everything was distributed equally, as would happen in Glaw Wood. The fish tasted slightly muddy, being a river fish, but the skin was crisp and Ysolda chewed it, bones and all, to mush.

The tea was another unfamiliar thing, the leaves and berries unlike anything she'd drunk before: bitterness chased by sweet. She never knew food could have such depth. It was clearly common in the queen's castle, because no one else looked like they were drinking the most delicious thing they had ever tasted.

'To sleep,' ordered the queen, when they had finished. 'We will not rest again until tomorrow's dawn. The wolves will wake us.'

The wolves were already asleep, though Tej's furry ears twitched towards the sound of her voice.

'I'm sure this does not need saying,' said the general to Ysolda and Sami. 'But if you try to leave, the wolves will find you. If you try anything while we sleep, the wolves will stop you. You'd be best advised to rest. Though you snored enough to wake the dead earlier,' she added to Ysolda.

Ysolda flushed as the Ryders laughed, and they all settled down on their mats, their cloaks bundled around them like blankets, the queen under the cloth of her shawl. Ysolda lay down too, and Sami turned his back to her, his head by her feet.

The mat was surprisingly comfortable, but Ysolda felt very awake. It seemed unnatural to sleep in the growing daylight, and her doze on wolfback had lasted hours, so now her blood was alive and singing. She wanted to walk, but the general's warning about the wolves was fresh in her mind. She didn't feel like trying to explain to a wolf she was only going for a stroll. She shifted so she could search the peak for Nara, but the hawk was either off hunting or in shadow.

'You're wiggling,' hissed Sami.

'Sorry,' mumbled Ysolda. 'Not tired.'

He sighed quietly. 'Me neither.'

This was all the encouragement Ysolda needed. As silently as she could, she moved so she was lying the same way as him.

'Your breath is tickling me,' he grumbled, rubbing his ear, but he didn't move away.

'I'm sorry you got caught,' said Ysolda. 'I wish I could have helped you.'

Sami's shoulders stiffened. 'It was Deepti's idea. I told her we wouldn't make it. The Ryders are too fast.'

'Not as fast as wolves.'

Sami shuddered. 'No. But only those travelling with the queen can ride them.'

'I'm beginning to like them.'

Sami turned towards her. Their faces were so close Ysolda went cross-eyed trying to look at him. 'Don't. They're only her pets. They're beasts to everyone else.'

'Do you always look after them?'

'I do whatever I'm told.' He paused. 'Why are you here? I heard they took you to the caves.'

'They did. I saw my sister, but the queen ordered me to come, to navigate.'

'I didn't know you could do that.'

Ysolda hesitated. 'I can't, exactly.'

'What do you mean?'

Ysolda paused, wondering whether to trust him. But he disliked the queen at least as much as her. 'Kore told me to pretend.'

'The Forgiver?'

'Yes.'

'So you don't know where we're going?'

'I do. Everyone in Glaw Wood knows the way to the End-World Wood. It's simple really – travel north-east until the land runs out. Then it's on an island, covered by fog and across the narrow sea. You have to wait for the tides to leave, the current is too strong else.'

'So the stuff about your tongue shrivelling or whatever . . .'

'A lie.'

Sami sucked in a breath. 'Careful, Glaw Wood girl.'

'I'm being careful, Lakes boy.'

Sami kicked her, and there was a warning whine from the pile of wolves. The two fell silent, waiting for the animals to quieten again.

In a smaller voice than ever, Sami said, 'Do you think we'll get back?'

'What?'

'To the castle.'

'I thought you wanted to be away from there.'

'I have nowhere else to go. Did the Forgiver tell you if I will?'

'No,' said Ysolda, truthfully. 'But I'm sure we shall. The queen seems to get what she wants.'

This seemed to comfort Sami, and his eyelids drooped. As he drifted off to sleep, he wriggled closer to Ysolda and linked his thumb around hers.

CHAPTER TWENTY-THREE

SLIP

Ysolda couldn't join Sami in sleep, which was how she learned that the general was a fine one to talk about snoring. She couldn't get comfortable, and every time she shifted, the wolves growled. The shadow of Nara swooped overhead, and Ysolda smiled, hearing the splosh of her hunting fish in the lake.

She held on to the hag stone, and thought about Hari, and Kore, and Eira, watching the day lighten from dawn's purple to pink, and finally to something close to a blue sky, the sun pale yellow as a sick chicken's egg yolk.

The wolves woke a few hours later. At their first waking yawn the queen pulled the shawl from her head and stood up. Her torc caught the sun and it glinted across the surrounding rocks.

'Up,' she said, and the Ryders rolled blearily from their mats. Dismantling their small camp took no time, and soon they were on the move again, Ysolda and the general on Ravi.

The landscape began to change further. The gentle hills gave way to sharper peaks, heather and gorse giving way to hardy, straggly trees hanging from the rock. The pack's pace barely slowed though the ground was unstable, rocks working free and tumbling behind them.

The weather around them struggled to make up its mind. A light rain passed over, not worth a scramble for oilskins in the saddle packs. Shafts of sunlight broke through the clouds in blades of brightness, and then the wind upped and blew the rain away. Perhaps this was usual in this place, and seeing as she claimed to be a wise navigator Ysolda knew she couldn't ask. But it felt wrong, watching the weather wipe itself clear and start its cycle anew, again and again.

Added to the lack of birds, it was easy to let Uncle's story echo in her mind. *The world is turning away from us. Turning on us. It would be better, and worse, if the queen does not fail.*

They took an incline that went on so long Ysolda lost count of the strides, the wolf's shoulder blades slicing through its fur in rolling mounds. The wind was fierce and she was glad of the general's shelter, the size and sturdiness of the wolf. She searched for Nara, but the hawk must be sailing higher in the air or waiting the gale out. She thought of Kore's proclamation that they would see the clouds as sea, but there were none, and however high, they were still far below the cloudline. Still, it was enough to turn her stomach when she looked down.

At the top, the general pulled the panting wolf to a stop. Ysolda peered around her body and looked down into a massive lake that echoed the sky, so vast she could not see across. Mist obscured the opposite bank, and the slope they stood atop was rocky and loose.

The queen pulled her wolf to a stop beside theirs. 'Mirror Lake.'

Ysolda scrambled to find words. 'Ah yes, I knew we would reach this today. Perhaps it would be best to make camp again this side before riding around?'

The queen's clever eyes burned into Ysolda's. 'We do not stop for night. And we do not go around. You said yourself, the most direct route, yes? And these are sea wolves, after all.'

'Yes, Queen Seren.'

'Yes,' said the woman to herself. By now the other two wolves had caught up, and the steam rose from their backs and their long red tongues as they panted.

'The hillside looks loose,' said the general, eyeing the sharp slope. 'Perhaps we could find a gentler descent.'

'Nonsense, Shiv,' scoffed the queen. 'We have encountered worse in the Marbled Hills. If you wish to find a gentler way, I will not wait.'

The queen spurred Tej into action. He took the scramble down at a sprint, leaping lithely from rock to rock. The boulders began to shift, smaller pebbles coming loose and running down the hillside, but the wolf outpaced them. Ysolda could feel the general's discomfort as she watched Seren and Tej disappear, and her face was set as she turned to speak to Cai and Ani. 'Quickly, before it slides. Watch your tongues.'

Ysolda hardly had time to tighten her grip before Ravi plunged after Tej. With the ground already unstable he had a harder time, the boulders slipping and sending them lurching down.

Ysolda's belly flipped, her teeth snapped down on the side of her tongue, and she realised what the general had meant. She curled it to the top of her mouth, gritted her teeth. The queen was already at the base of the hill, crouched on her wolf's back, feet splayed for grip.

It felt, for the first time, that Ravi was not entirely in control. They seemed to fly from boulder to boulder, barely touching the shifting ground, and Ysolda pressed her eyes closed as she saw the lake rising to meet them, too fast—

Ravi landed with a thump that jarred every bone, and he let out a small whine. The general leant forward and smoothed his muzzle. 'Good boy, Ravi. *Shanti*, peace, boy.'

Tej had already waded out to the shallows of Mirror Lake and begun to swim. Ysolda looked uncertainly at the general's profile, but she made no move to follow her leader. All her attention was on the wolves and their riders now descending the slope.

A stone hit Ysolda's shoulder and she twisted, seeing Cai's and Ani's wolves skidding down the hill. Sami's face was blanched and he gripped Cai, whose jaw was locked hard shut. As if in slow motion, Ysolda saw a larger boulder free as Ani's wolf hit it, sending the animal's legs skewing. It yelped as the boulder began to roll, and there was a sickening sound of bones breaking.

'No!' The general leaped from Ravi's back and struck his hindquarters so he ran clear of the falling rocks. Ysolda clutched tight to his fur, just managing to stay seated. The general was ducking rocks, scrambling up towards the injured wolf with frightening agility, but it was clear the wolf's back leg was broken, and it fell to the ground, throwing Ani clear. The woman hit the rocks and bounced unnaturally, once, twice, and came to a halt at the shoreline, boulders and pebbles still falling around her.

Ravi plunged into the water. It was icy, knocking the breath from Ysolda, but they and Cai's wolf had moved just in time. The boulder struck another and began a landslide, the hillside dislodging and rushing forward like a wave, slamming into the water and sending a shower over their heads. Ysolda lost sight of the general a moment, then saw her running over the avalanche like a skimming stone, keeping her feet.

'Shiv!' The queen had turned Tej back, not waiting for him to reach the newly extended shore before leaping off him to the pile of rocks created by the landslide. There was no sign of Ani or the wolf.

The queen fell to her knees and threw aside one of the rocks. She was trying to dig them out, though dust was still rising in threatening plumes from the hillside. 'Hurry! *Jaldi, jaldi!*'

The general was barely panting. She whistled Ravi back to shore and kneeled to join the hunt. Trembling with shock, Ysolda dismounted Ravi and began to dig. She couldn't lift the larger stones, but Cai and the general used their spear hilts as levers, and Sami and Ysolda pulled out the rolling pebbles that filled the gaps.

'Here!' The queen's shout made Ysolda jump. The rest of them hurried to her side. Her brown skin was stained with dust, the gold of her torc dull and her braid grey as an old woman's. Ysolda could see her fingernails were bleeding, some bent and torn, but the queen continued to dig around the scarlet of a cloak. They joined her, uncovering the rider's arms, torso, head and legs, and at last heaved out Ani.

Ysolda swallowed bitterness. It was clear she was dead. Cai let out a small sob, but then a yelp issued from somewhere to their left, and the queen did not hesitate. She threw herself back to digging, all of them working together in a grim silence. The other wolves were pacing the bank, showing more agitation than Ysolda had ever seen in them. The sombre group removed another boulder and the yelp became louder, so sorrowful it brought instant tears to Ysolda's eyes. The wolves on the shore began to howl.

They uncovered the wolf's side and flanks. It was still alive, but clearly in agony. Ysolda knew that wild animals were usually at their most dangerous while in pain, but the wolf lay docile as a puppy, looking up at the queen with baleful eyes. Ysolda glanced between the animal and the wolf queen, and saw Seren was crying silently, glassy tears rolling down her dust-streaked cheeks.

'There is nothing to be done,' she said. 'General?'

Lips a thin line, the general stepped forward, spear in hand. The queen pressed her forehead to the wolf's so they were close as could be, and whispered to it in an unending stream. Ysolda realised what was about to happen and squeezed her eyes shut, pressing her hands to her ears. But still she heard the swoosh of the spear, the final yelp, the surviving wolves howling at the sky.

CHAPTER TWENTY-FOUR

SKY BURIAL

They took Ani's cloak, the wolf's left incisor. Both were removed by the queen herself, both held reverentially up to the sky, and the Ryders bowed their heads. Seren's face was pinched as she washed the tooth in the water of Mirror Lake, and strung it on to her belt. Ani's cloak was rolled and placed in the general's saddlebag.

'We do not have time for full rites,' said Seren. 'Nor the wood for a pyre. Ani would understand. A sky burial, to return them.'

The general's eyes were bright, but not a single tear fell as she nodded and ordered Ysolda and Sami to fetch water to wash the bodies. Ysolda filled flask after flask while the general helped Cai pile rocks into a narrow platform. On this, they laid Ani's mat, and then Ani.

It took all of them to pull the wolf to the platform. Its fur was coarse under Ysolda's fingers, still warm. They poured water over them, the bodies steaming slightly in the chill air. The other wolves continued to howl their mourning, and the queen sat cross-legged, one hand pressed to her heart, eyes closed. She seemed to be chanting, too quiet for Ysolda to hear. A prayer, maybe.

Ysolda had never seen a sky burial before. It was oddly beautiful, not to destroy the bodies with fire or conceal them with earth, but to leave them out in the wild for weather and animals to take them – if there were any animals around. Ysolda had seen none but the wolves and Nara, occasionally skimming the corner of her vision.

'Is this a Lakes tradition?' she murmured, edging closer to Sami.

'It's Seren's. Brought from the north of her first realm. She takes rites from everywhere, uses what she likes, discards the rest.'

Cai hissed, and the boy fell silent. Ysolda considered this statement. It was as Uncle had said, about her names – Seren possessed a place and its culture as much as it possessed her. It seemed a good way to rule, if there were such a thing. It made sense to Ysolda, anyway.

The queen opened her eyes. She fixed them on the general. 'Shiv,' she murmured. 'Shiv, I—'

'You did what you must,' said the general, and with a

188

jolt Ysolda realised the queen was asking for forgiveness. She remembered the look of peace that had washed over her face when Kore had absolved them of future sins. The queen blamed herself for Ani's and Bala's deaths. *And so she should*, thought Ysolda. *The general warned her it was dangerous*. But looking at the absolute devastation on Seren's face, it would take a harder heart than Ysolda's not to soften a little.

The general placed her hand on Seren's shoulder a moment, a tender gesture, more as a friend than a warrior to her queen. '*Shanti*,' she said. 'Peace. Remember why we are here.'

Seren closed her eyes and took a deep breath.

Then her eyes snapped open. 'On.'

The water was cold as stone. It struck Ysolda's ankles like pebbles, and her teeth began to chatter immediately. The bulk and strength of the wolf meant they were high out of the water, but still their feet trailed in the icy Mirror Lake. Ysolda's boots were slung around her neck, and she regarded the general's, hanging over the woman's shoulder by their leather laces. They were constructed of tanned leather and the soles were reinforced with an unfamiliar, springy-seeming wood. The whole structure of them was so solid and certain, like the woman herself. But there were signs of softening, in the wrinkles across the top and the laces beginning to fray.

The general, too, seemed gentler since leaving her soldier at the base of the hill behind them. She'd helped Ysolda up on to Ravi's back herself and told her to let her hair down to keep her ears warm as they crossed the lake. She and the queen had done the same, their black hair falling in shimmering sheets behind them. There was no sound but the pant of the wolves, the splash of their legs paddling, Ysolda's teeth clattering together. The crossing took an age, and soon enough Ysolda couldn't feel her feet any more, tendrils of cold licking up her legs.

She was amazed by the strength of the wolves, how Ravi's body was still warm despite hours submerged in the lake. Sea wolves had crossed to the Isles from the Thawless Circle, and now Ysolda considered this, the crossing their ancestors had made, swimming all that way. The distance she had already travelled from Glaw Wood was far enough.

It was nearing dusk when they arrived at the far bank. They dismounted to allow the wolves to shake themselves dry and stretch, and Cai started a small fire to dry their feet. Ysolda's hands were so cold she could not replace her shoes, and the general did so for her, adding a pair of thick woollen socks that pulled up and over her calves.

'Thank you,' said Ysolda through chattering teeth, and the woman shrugged off her gratitude. She murmured something to the queen, who turned her imperious gaze on Ysolda a moment, before looking back at the general and nodding.

The general pulled Ani's cloak from the wolf's pack and slung it around Ysolda's shoulders. Ysolda froze, feeling the hostile eyes of Cai, the shocked gaze of Sami, as the general pulled the cloak closed around her neck with the fine brass clip.

'No sense you freezing to death,' she said gruffly. 'We need you.'

She meant it kindly, but it sounded like a threat to Ysolda. It reminded her how precarious her position was in the group – it was all built on the lie that she couldn't simply tell them where the End-World Wood was. Sami looked at her warily, and she knew he was thinking the same.

She ducked her head so the general could not see the fear in her face, and gathered Kore's words to her. *She likes to believe people are special. She thinks she is, so she surrounds herself with the best.* Ysolda was one of these special people. She should start acting like it.

She lifted her chin and met the general's eyes. 'We should go.'

'Yes,' said Seren. 'Which way?'

Ysolda scanned the sky. The first star was alight, showing North. 'There.'

'My queen,' said the general tautly, 'those are—'

'Thane Boreal's lands.' The queen nodded gravely. 'We knew we would meet them eventually. Night is best to greet whatever comes. Still, arm the children.'

Cai thrust a short-handled spear at Sami, and Ysolda was given a small knife drawn out from the general's boot. It was metal, weighty and engraved with unfamiliar script, the hilt wrapped with leather for grip.

'I'll be wanting that back,' she said. 'It was a gift from my husband, upon the birth of our daughter.'

'Interesting choice,' said Ysolda, before she could stop herself.

The flash of a smile. 'We were that sort of family.'

They climbed back astride the wolves, and ascended the bank to find the landscape again changed. Ysolda had heard of the Kalti Forest, which dwarfed Glaw Wood in size and was the stronghold of Thane Boreal and his Kalti army, but she never thought she'd see it. Beneath the arriving stars it looked the stuff of nightmares, though she knew it was only a wood.

Endless, dense pines, unlike the soft, spreading trees Ysolda was used to, jutted out spikily before them, the darkness sharpening them to menace against the dimming horizon. None of the fading daylight reached beneath the canopy, which was shadowed as a cave. Ysolda scanned its boundary, stretching as far as the eye could see, but there were no guards posted at the border. Thane Boreal's reputation was enough to keep people away, just as Seren's did from the Lakes.

'Stay close,' said the queen. 'Keep your weapons to hand, but not in them – we want a chance to explain we are only passing through. Peace has been long between us, and Thane Boreal will not wish for a fight.'

The general gave a disbelieving snort that only Ysolda could hear.

'But above all, if we encounter anyone, we do not tell them we are making for the End-World Wood. We say as little as possible, and at most only that we wish to pass through to search for my daughter. We can appeal to his humanity.'

'If it exists,' murmured the general.

Ysolda looked overhead in time to see Nara swooping fast and low for the cover of the trees. The hawk would be as glad as she to arrive in a forest again, however unfamiliar. Knowing Nara could stick closer by made Ysolda feel braver, and she slid the knife into her belt, hoping she would not have cause to use it.

CHAPTER TWENTY-FIVE

THE MUTE FOREST

In such dense canopy there should have been the chatter of birds, the whoops of predators and the furtive scurryings of prey. But it was so silent they might have been underground. They travelled single file through the forest, weaving a route between the close-set trunks, Ravi at the fore, Tej in the middle, and Haddi at the rear. The wolves' ears swivelled, searching for sound, but none came. Only the faint patter of rain arrived overhead, scant drops reaching the root-ruckled ground.

Ysolda's jaw ached with gritting her teeth, expecting the sudden flapping of a bird, the cracking of branches, the cry of an attack – but though she stayed braced, hand straying often to the knife in her belt, there was nothing to break the tension. Nara was either far above them or extra quiet.

The wolves' night vision made them sure-footed as darkness fell in earnest, but there was hesitation even in them, felt through the taut muscle of their backs, the panting breaths that grew and shrunk their ribcages.

On they slunk through the mute forest, the wolves so careful Ysolda could have closed her eyes and thought herself floating. She looked up, hoping for a glimpse of light, but the moon was obscured doubly through cloud and canopy.

It would not be silent here for Hari. What stories would these trees tell her, what warnings would they have? Did they know where the animals had gone, or were they confused and afraid, only knowing something was deeply wrong?

Ysolda thought of her sister in her stone prison with Uncle and Aunty and their terror, their mutterings about mythic powers and the end of the world. She wished that her sister was free and beside her, or that they were both at home in Glaw Wood, stoking the fire as Sorrell stretched out before it and Nara tore noisy strips from a piece of fish. The image was so strong Ysolda could almost feel the warmth of the flames on her toes, and a wave of homesickness crashed over her.

'What was that?' whispered the general.

Ysolda had not known she'd spoken.

'Nothing,' she said. 'I was . . .' She paused, perilously

close to sharing her feelings with this warrior. 'Thinking about home.'

'Glaw Wood,' said the general. 'A wet place.'

'No wetter than the Lakes,' bristled Ysolda, and the general laughed softly.

'This whole country is drenched. At home, we have a rainy season that fills our rivers and grows our crops, and a dry one where we can enjoy them. Here it is rain, rain, rain, and when it is not raining, it is cold.'

Ysolda bit back her retort. In a softer voice, the general said, 'Your sister will be freed when we find the Anchorite. The queen is a woman of her word.'

'Yes,' said Ysolda, but more uncertainly than she'd meant to.

The general's back stiffened. 'She is the most honourable person I know.'

'You . . .' Ysolda hesitated but curiosity drove her on. 'You seem to be friends.'

'We grew as sisters,' said the general. 'We were set on our paths as children. She to be the Raani, I a Senapati.'

'Senapati?'

'Army lord. We were both girls determined to prove ourselves in families of men. We succeeded.' Pride sharpened her tone. 'She has succeeded beyond anything anyone dreamed – she united our realm as one. It is a vast place, with many customs and rituals, many languages. But we all serve our raani. And she may yet be the saviour of the world. You should be glad to serve her.'

'I don't serve—'

'We are all in her service, Glaw Wood girl. Don't forget you live by her mercy.'

'She needs me though,' said Ysolda, wishing she did not have to hold on to the woman in order to stay atop the wolf.

'That may be, but I hope for your sake you understand the stakes at play here, child. We are not on a simple journey. This is a mission, one that holds all our fates in the balance. Thane Boreal is the smallest danger we face.'

'You mean the happenings?'

The general turned her head sharply, so Ysolda could see her profile. 'What do you know of happenings?'

Ysolda thought rapidly. Her instinct was to let it go, but her curiosity burned. And what had Kore told her, about being special, being a mystery? It would not hurt to act a little wiser than she was. 'I know the lack of birds is strange. I know the red storm was wrong. I know there is a power growing along the lines of the earth that threatens—'

'Hush,' spat the general, so quiet it was barely more than an exhale through clenched teeth. 'You would do well to focus on the task at hand. How long does this forest go on?'

'Until the coast,' said Ysolda. Like Glaw Wood, the trees would last until the ground became too sandy to grip their roots. And then, across the tidal sea, there was the island where the last of an ancient wood grew. Her faith in these facts anchored her.

'Let's hope Thane Boreal has left with the birds.'

With no landmarks to lead them, and no view of the stars, Ysolda was relying on the wolves' instincts for north. She drifted into an uneasy sleep, and woke to the same unnatural silence. The sky began to lighten, showing the position of sunrise and she corrected them further east, so they would reach the coast before the land broadened. Eira's map was stuck fast in her mind, and Ysolda felt a grudging gratitude towards the girl.

She rolled her head, hearing her neck click, her back sore from hours on wolfback, and scanned the surrounding trees. With a rush of joy, she spotted Nara, but the bird was acting oddly, shifting from one foot to another on a high branch. Ysolda's gaze snagged on the trunk of the tree, and before she could check herself, she gasped, 'Stop!'

'Hush!' snapped the queen and the general in unison, but Ysolda shook her head, desperately reaching for the reins. 'No, look! Stop!'

The wolf pulled up short, and Ysolda fell from its back in her haste to reach the nearest tree. She reached up the rough trunk, and traced the symbol written there.

A word: *marbh*.

'What language is it?' The queen was beside her, moving on feet silent as her wolf's.

'Ogham,' said Ysolda, eyes stuck to the shape.

'What does it say?'

'Dead.'

The queen leaned closer. 'But the tree lives.'

Ysolda searched it for signs of sickness, but found none. The trunk was not hollow, and the needles were strong and green. 'Yes.'

'So? Does it have other meanings?'

'Maybe endings. But it is quite clear. Spelt, not meant.' Ysolda frowned. The definite markings were strange. Usually Ogham was written to gesture at words and meanings, not to spell them letter by letter.

'What is it?' The general had dismounted too, and her hand was on her spear.

'These lines are a word,' said the queen. '"Dead". Our navigator can read it, but not interpret. Half-useful.'

'Well, it's nothing good,' said Ysolda defensively, and the women exchanged impatient glances.

'We are in Thane Boreal's forest,' said Seren. 'Of course

it is nothing good.'

'We use this alphabet at winter solstice,' continued Ysolda. 'But usually there is room for change. It will say ending, but within that is a beginning: of the season, growth. But this –' she tapped the trunk – 'this spells the letters. M-a-r-b-h. Dead.'

'And here,' said a voice behind them. Cai, speaking for the first time since they'd left Ani at the lakeside. 'What does this say?'

He and Sami were still on wolfback, their eyes level with another symbol.

Ysolda moved closer, trying not to flinch from the wolf as she read the word aloud. 'All.'

'And here?' The general pointed to another tree.

'Dead, again.' Ysolda scanned the trees. They were naturally seeded, and did not grow in ordered lines, but each tree had its place, none growing too close to another, so it was easy to see the pattern: the same two words, repeated over and over. 'All dead.'

'Not all,' said a voice, deep and low, from high above their heads. And before Ysolda could so much as blink, men dropped from the sky.

CHAPTER TWENTY-SIX

BOREAL

Ropes fell like a web over them. The wolves howled, their legs caught in nets that sent them stumbling to the ground. Nara screeched as two men seized the queen, who snarled in protest, kneeing one hard in the stomach and backhanding the other across the face.

But more men followed the first, maybe two dozen flooding the clearing, and Ysolda was held in a vice-like grip, the unmistakable shouts of Kalti men in her ears. She didn't even have time to reach for the knife in her belt.

She was forced to her knees and looked up in time to see Sami and Cai pushed to theirs too by men patterned all over in blue and black dyes, their pale skin shining luminous through the markings. She whistled Nara off, for the hawk looked ready to plunge, and watched the queen still fighting her captors fiercely. The general was free, wielding her spear in wide circles around her, keeping all at a distance. But then the man holding Ysolda shouted a warning, and Ysolda felt cold flint at her neck, sharp and piercing.

The queen and the general paused their resistance, and at a signal from the queen the general threw down her spear with a growl of frustration. Seren clicked her tongue and the wolves stopped fighting, though their eyes were still wide and white-rimmed with frenzy.

'Free them,' she said imperiously. 'They will not attack you.'

Three men approached the general nervously, and it gave Ysolda a strange satisfaction to see how they seemed afraid of her even unarmed. She hissed at the man binding her hands, and he flinched. The flint was still at Ysolda's neck, and she swallowed carefully. The Kalti men spoke to one another in their thick dialect, and a blindfold of what smelled like hare pelt was wrapped over her eyes.

'Up,' said the man holding her, his accent familiar from the traders who visited Glaw Wood's coast on their way to and from the Kalti's sisterland across the ocean, Ulaid. Ysolda obeyed as best she could, but her legs were weak with shock, the blindfold unbalancing her. After so much silence, so long hearing only women in command, the shouts of all these men were overwhelming.

With the man still holding her shoulder tightly, she was

forced into a brisk walk. Behind, she could hear the queen protesting her restraint, the whining wolves ordered to obey these strangers. They walked and walked, Ysolda's limbs clumsy and her head light, the hand on her shoulder at times holding her up. The ground was uneven and soon began a relentless rise that made her legs ache. Just as she was thinking she couldn't walk another step, and that she would never again curse riding on wolfback, they stopped.

Ysolda sniffed the air. There was no smell of woodsmoke, no sign they were near a settlement, though the Kalti men had kept up a solid wall of chatter that filled her ears. Maybe there were more voices now, but she was disorientated, and when the hand released her shoulder she fell again to her knees, her hands meeting a sharp bed of pine needles.

She heard others forced down next to her, the queen saying loudly, 'Let go,' and the general grunting. She felt an elbow next to hers, small and pointed, and guessed Sami was beside her. She leaned slightly against him, and he echoed her movement, his weight comforting. The boy was shaking, and she tried to control the chatter of her own teeth.

The sound around them reached an excited crescendo, which ceased so suddenly it must have been on a signal. And then a deep voice spoke with such authority, Ysolda was in no doubt as to who it was.

'Do you know who you have brought me? The wolves are perhaps a giveaway.' Thane Boreal sounded amused. 'But what must you think of our manners, Raani. Untie her.'

'I'll be glad to have my sight back too, Boreal,' snapped the queen. 'Or are you as ugly as they say?'

Thane Boreal laughed. 'You be the judge, Raani.'

'Seren,' said the queen. 'Queen Seren, on these lands.'

'On the contrary,' said Thane Boreal. 'On these lands you are no one. You live only by my mercy.'

'A famously thin thing. Release my companions.'

'I don't think so. That is General Shivani, is it not?'

'At least let them have their sight.'

Ysolda's blindfold was removed, and she blinked rapidly, trying to clear her blurred vision. They were in a dipped clearing ringed by uprooted trees that lay in a circle around them like shattered walls. The wolves were tied to their trunks, and Nara had the sense to have stayed far off. Sami blinked from her right, and Cai kneeled, silent on her left. Beyond him were the queen, on her feet now, and the general, who was glaring at the man standing atop a flat rock at the centre of the clearing.

He was short and broad as the shield at his side, clothed in furs. His chest, arms and face were covered in intricate swirls and spirals of blue and black, and Ysolda was minded of the Forgiver's cave, the shapes seeming to come to life.

His hair and beard were long and matted, a bright copper that matched the torc around his neck. Scars twisted his mouth into a permanent sneer, and he was not at all ugly. He looked exactly as the Kalti lord should – wild and strong and battletorn. He and the queen were regarding each other with matching expressions of interest and suspicion.

'Give them water,' said Thane Boreal. 'Are you hungry?'

'Not for Kalti food,' said the queen, and Boreal laughed again.

'You mustn't believe the rumours. It is not all gruel. They would have us believe you had teeth sharp as your wolves'.'

'Maybe not, but my bite is.'

'Not your wit, alas,' said Boreal as his men stepped forward with flagons. Ysolda drank gratefully, the stale liquid spilling down her chin. 'Why are you in my forest, Queen?'

'Passing through, only,' said Seren. 'Though there seems not to be much left of it.' She looked around at the uprooted trees. 'I would have explained, had your men given me a chance.'

'You must forgive them,' said Boreal in mock apology. 'Although you'll admit you do not present the friendliest presence.' He gestured at the wolves, which stood placid as dogs under the trees, eyes trained on Seren, awaiting her command. 'Passing through to where? What interests you on the western shore?' He narrowed his eyes. 'Are you expecting boats?'

'No,' said Seren. 'We are looking for someone. My daughter, Eira.'

Boreal's fiery eyebrows lifted in surprise. 'The wolf queen has a pup?'

'She has gone missing and was seen heading for Kalti lands. Have you seen her?'

Boreal looked at his assembled warriors, a few of whom shook their heads. 'No Lakes girl has come this way.'

'Perhaps she skirted the forest,' said the queen. 'Will you permit us to continue?'

Boreal narrowed his eyes. 'Queen, do you not notice anything amiss?'

The queen looked around scathingly. 'The hospitality is lacking. You could try wearing a shirt.'

'If you are unaware that something is wrong in the forest, I would question you are truly the wolf queen at all.'

'It is silent,' said Ysolda, before she could think better of it. Boreal's eyes snapped on to her, and she spoke to the ground. 'No birds. No deer. And the Ogham, on the trees. They speak of death.'

'Who are you?' asked Boreal.

'A servant girl only,' said Seren.

'I asked you, who are you?' repeated Boreal. 'Clearly you are not from the Lakes, or another of her realms.'

'A servant,' said Ysolda. 'From Glaw Wood.'

'You're extending your reach then, Raani,' said Boreal. 'Should I be concerned?'

'She trespassed,' lied Seren. 'She is paying penance in service.'

'Are you sure,' said Boreal, 'that she is not one of your stolen gifted?'

CHAPTER TWENTY-SEVEN

STRONGHOLD

'I don't know what you mean.' The queen did not so much as blink, but Boreal's gaze was hard and sharp as the flint at his waist.

'Yes, you do.' Boreal snapped his fingers at a nearby man, who stepped forward out of the rough ring the Kaltis had formed around them. 'Tell them what you know, Elgin.'

'We've seen you.' The man addressed Seren directly, his accent thicker than Boreal's. 'Taking them from beyond your borders. Listeners, green-touches, dowsers and seers. Any and all gifted, stolen and taken to your castle, where they are held under rock and surrounded by gems that quieten their powers.'

'I have never taken a Kalti,' said Seren hotly.

'Maybe,' said Boreal. 'But what do you want with all those people, Queen? I am not a fool, and you should not take me for one.'

The circle drew a little tighter, and Seren glanced at her wolves, who let out a warning growl.

'None of us wants a fight,' said Boreal lightly, hand resting on his flint. 'But I do want an answer.'

'I need them,' said Seren. 'The growers, the healers.'

'You have the best, from all over your realms. I heard you are looking for someone – not your daughter.' He held up a hand to stop Seren interrupting. 'And however much you pretend, I know you noticed the silence of the forest. I know you wonder why we are meeting in this clearing of uprooted trees and not in my fabled longhouse atop Fallow Brae.'

'That, I do wonder,' said Seren.

'It is not safe,' said Boreal simply. 'Not any more. Even here, we are at risk.' He looked directly at the queen. 'We leave each other alone, but we know of each other's strongholds. Your castle of broken ships, my longhouse of shields. And you also know Fallow Brae is home to a henge, a circle of stones that has long protected our stronghold.

'But a few weeks ago, strange things began to happen. Shaking of the earth, sinking beneath our floors. Toxins in the wells, and then the trees . . .' He looked around them, almost fearfully. 'The trees began to poison us.'

Seren snorted, and Boreal's face was suddenly furious. He rounded once more on Ysolda. 'You, Glaw Wood girl. Have you heard of such a thing? Has it happened at your home? Sap turning to acid, woodsmoke like venomous gas. Even the needles grew sharper.'

'No,' said Ysolda, 'but there have been quakes. My home was destroyed.'

Thane Boreal stepped forward, and she flinched, but he only laid a heavy hand on her shoulder. She could smell the berries crushed to make his ink, the musk of the furs he wore.

'I am sorry. It is an awful thing, to be forced to leave your land.' His eyes flashed again at Seren. 'Some people do not understand. They collect countries like tokens.'

'Do not pretend to care about the girl,' said Seren. 'She is not stupid. She knows you only speak so because you believe she is something special. Well, she is not, so you can drop the act.'

'That is another lie,' said Boreal. 'Elgin told me that when he held a flint to her neck, you ordered your dogs –' he looked at the general to show he included her in this description – 'to cease their attack. What is this girl to you?'

'She's . . .' Seren hesitated. 'Well, she's—'

'I'm Eira's friend,' said Ysolda. She did not know why she was helping the wolf queen, but there was something about Boreal, his kindliness, that she trusted even less than

Seren's ruthlessness. 'I'm here to convince her to return with us.'

Boreal frowned. The hand on her shoulder contracted, pressing a tender place that made her eyes water. 'Are you lying, child?'

'No,' said Ysolda, balling her fists.

'You're not gifted?'

'No,' said Ysolda, and this at least was truth. Boreal released her.

'More's the pity. Ours have long passed, or fled.'

'From your poison trees?' said Seren.

'I can show you if you wish?' snapped Boreal. 'Elgin, bring me a stick of firewood. We can leave you alone with the smoke and see what you think of it.' His voice thickened. 'Hundreds, I lost. I had to abandon my longhouse to the dead and dying. We sent our women and children along what we thought was a safe path to the sea, a route that has long served and protected us.

'But even there, the firewood throttled them. Mushrooms that should be safe stuck in their throats. Berries we used for pies burned their tongues.' The grief in Boreal's voice was raw and deep as the Rhyg. 'And then we realised that route lay between the Fallow Brae henge and the Arbor Henge.'

Seren let out a small gasp, and Boreal nodded grimly. 'Now you understand.'

'And the marked trees,' said the queen. 'They too are in line with Arbor henge?'

'It is happening all over. The fenlands are sinking further, and the eels have grown fangs and claws. Our brothers in Ulaid report quakes and storms. It has begun, and you are not the only one who believes they hold the key.'

Seren's breath was coming in brief pants. She looked, for the first time, afraid.

'So you know, Raani,' said Boreal. 'I do not believe for a second you are passing through in search of your daughter. Maybe it is a girl you seek, but she has long run dry of blood.'

Tension filled the clearing. Ysolda knew he was talking about the Anchorite, though she had not taken the Kaltis for superstitious people. They were famously straight-talking, preferring to settle scores with swords over stories.

'The trees,' said Seren. 'You did this, searching for her?'

Ysolda looked at the murdered trees and realised that Thane Boreal had ordered them slain. He too was searching for the Anchorite, seeking her in the roots of his forest. Perhaps this was why the trees had turned against them.

Ysolda caught herself. Could trees do such a thing? Turn their berries to poison?

Thane Boreal's eyes were dark with fury. 'I did not know it had begun. I thought we had more time. But you understand, Raani. I cannot have competition.'

His hand twitched, and Ysolda's mouth became dry. He was going to kill them all.

'Now!' shouted Seren, and as suddenly as they'd been captured, chaos broke out once more. Cai kicked Ysolda sideways as arrows shot across the clearing. A rough hand tangled in her hair, but a moment later there was a cry of pain, and Ysolda looked in time to see Nara's beak drawing blood from the Kalti man's arm. She wrenched herself free, crouching low, her hand instinctively reaching for the general's borrowed blade.

Sami was cowering nearby, and she lunged for him, using her body to shield his as they crawled forward, seeking shelter. The pine needles pierced their hands, and she heard the wolves snarling, the vicious crunch of teeth on bone.

Two thick legs obstructed their way, and Ysolda saw the glint of metal as the man prepared to strike, but she kicked out, swiping with the knife. The man roared as the blade sank into his calf. Adrenaline pulsed through her like panic, and she felt sick as the blade came back bloody, but she did not hesitate. She yanked Sami into a hollow formed by a caved-in root and positioned herself before him, knife ready.

Nara swooped fast and low on to her shoulder, bruising the skin with her talons as she landed. Ysolda felt her trembling, and she was shaking herself as she watched the queen, Cai and the general fight back to back, the wolves picking off Boreal's men one by one.

Ysolda had never seen a real fight before. There was so much blood: on the ground, on her hand, on the faces of the fighters. She wanted to look away, but it was mesmeric, the fluid rhythm of the spears jabbing, the claws swiping, the arrows bouncing or embedding loosely into the wolves' flanks. One wolf bore down on Boreal, and he held it off with his bare hands, roaring into its jaws.

It was easy to believe the general was the greatest warrior in the world. Her spear in one hand, a stolen Kalti's sword in another, she ducked and spun, anticipating each attack. Her focus was absolute, but when she spotted Ysolda hidden in the clearing, her expression softened ever so slightly. She shouted something to the queen, who howled, 'Tej!'

Her wolf, the largest, batted aside three Kalti men and stormed to her side, followed by Ravi. Seren swung herself up, lay back flat to avoid another arrow, and then rode the wolf straight towards the hollow. Before Ysolda could react or reach for Sami, the queen's wolf had dragged her out by her leg, its teeth only grazing her skin, and flipped her over its head.

The world turned upside down. Ysolda felt like she was flying. Nara wheeled free and an arrow grazed Ysolda's palm but she barely felt it, her shock was so great, her body

217

and brain unable to keep up with what her eyes were seeing.

A long, strong arm reached for her and stopped her arc. She thudded down hard in front of the queen, nearly sliding from the wolf's back but held steady by Seren's grip.

'Down, Glaw Wood girl!'

Ysolda recognised the general's voice, turned in time to see a host of arrows taking aim at them. And then General Shivani, face set and determined, launched herself into the air, spear deflecting some of the missiles, more than half a dozen arrows hitting her body as it twisted to protect Ysolda and Seren. Perhaps Ysolda imagined it, but she thought the woman's eyes found hers, thought she saw her mouth form a soft *oh*.

'No!' Ysolda's shout was worse than useless. There were so many arrows, sharp and merciless. General Shivani was dead before she hit the ground.

'Stop!' she shouted, desperate for Seren to save the general though it was too late, for them to at least rescue Sami, who ran, reaching out towards them in a panicked, last-ditch effort to escape the Kaltis. But the queen urged the wolf on, trampling the boy, and leaving the blood-soaked clearing behind them, screams and howls rapidly becoming echoes in the doomed forest.

CHAPTER TWENTY-EIGHT

PURSUIT

She's dead. We left her. We left him. The words repeated over and over in Ysolda's head as uprooted trees sped past and the last of the arrows ceased reaching them. Louder and louder they grew, and it was not until Seren shouted in her ear, 'Shut *up*,' that Ysolda realised she was speaking them aloud.

'The general—'

'We could do nothing.'

'And Sami? We left him,' said Ysolda numbly. 'The wolf, it trampled him.'

'He got in the way,' said Seren, and Ysolda remembered all over again who she was, what she was. A woman who ruled by removing or ignoring obstacles, even when they were scared boys reaching for safety.

'We left all of them,' said Ysolda.

'We did what must be done.' Seren spurred Tej on faster with a harsh whistle, Ravi keeping close behind. 'They knew what was at stake. Every sacrifice must be made. You heard what Boreal told us. You saw the red sky. This is not about some servant boy, or even all the gifted in the land. It is bigger than us all. Now shut up your crying and tell me where to go.'

Hiccupping, Ysolda searched the sky. There was Nara, silhouetted against the dusk. It was moving to evening again – they had been nearly a full day in the Kalti Forest, and there was no sign of the felled trees thinning. She corrected their course north-east. Thane Boreal's quest to find the Anchorite was clear – every tree on the horizon was down, the roots reaching for the sky like Sami's hands—

'He knows,' muttered the queen. 'More than I guessed at. Perhaps he has scouts even now. But he cannot be told, can he?' she said, and Ysolda realised she was talking to her. 'The curse, the hold over your tongue. No one can tell him.'

It sounded so ridiculous repeated back to her Ysolda nearly laughed. But instead she nodded, feeling Seren's hot sigh of relief hit her neck. Ysolda's mouth felt sour.

'We have the advantage still,' said Seren. 'But he will be in pursuit.'

'The general,' said Ysolda, closing her eyes. The speed

the trees flew past was making her feel sick, but against her lids was the image of Sami with his hand raised, the general and Cai swinging their weapons.

'Shiv is the fiercest fighter I've ever known,' said the queen, but emotion filled her voice. 'It was the right death for her, in the heat of battle.'

But it was a sacrifice made for me. Ysolda knew the general's last act had been to save her, to save her queen. Bile filled her throat, and she heaved her guts on to the ground.

They rode until steam rose from Tej in the cooling night, stopping only when his stride became slower, his breathing hard. Seren dismounted, Ysolda dropping unsteadily beside her. They were in a gully, chalky water running around their ankles, and Ysolda didn't know if she had been too taken in by Boreal's tale, but she thought she felt sharp pangs around her feet, like the water was full of tiny teeth.

'Look,' she said, pointing upstream. A cloudy-eyed fish was floating belly up in the sluggish, shallow current. Its scales were faded in places, like it had been rubbed with sandpaper. In horror, Ysolda saw her hawk plunge for the fish, and she shouted, 'Nara, no!'

The hawk caught herself in a great snap of wings, hovering a moment before alighting on the bank and tilting her head mournfully at Ysolda.

'Nara?'

Ysolda turned slowly, heart pounding. The queen's eyes were narrowed.

'I thought a hawk was following us. Yours, is she?'

There was no point denying it. 'Yes.'

Ysolda waited for the blow to fall, but Seren only grunted. 'You did not need to keep it hidden.'

Ysolda's heart thudded. Another dull-eyed fish floated past their feet.

'Let's not linger here,' said Seren. 'She can ride with us. I imagine she needs a rest.'

Nara flew gratefully on to Ysolda's shoulder. Though her talons stung without her shoulder guard, Ysolda felt so soothed by the weight she didn't care that the hawk was drawing blood.

Now she saw why they had brought Ravi too. Seren leaped lightly on to the second wolf's back and reached out her hand wordlessly to Ysolda, who used a nearby stump to climb up, this time behind the queen. She shook her feet to get the water off, and a droplet landed on her hand. A welt sprang up immediately, like a sandfly bite.

'We drink and eat only what we brought from the Lakes,' said Seren. 'We have enough.'

The wolf whined, lifting its paws.

'All right, Ravi,' soothed the queen. 'We're going.'

Ysolda was uncertain about holding on to the queen, but Seren pulled her arms impatiently around her waist and spurred the wolf into a run, leaving the dying stream behind.

Tej trailed them, exhausted, the two animals howling to each other to stay within calling distance. Without the extra load, Tej slowly recovered his strength and was soon near them once more, breathing restored to an easy pant.

Stroking a sleeping Nara, Ysolda turned to watch the wolf, his docile face no longer holding the same terror for her. It was easy to think of them as dogs after all, obeying their master. She thought of their companions, dead by the lake and in the clearing. She thought of Sami and had to stop, because the awfulness of it was so much it made her thoughts turn to stone, her mind unable to linger on his face, his small, dark hand outstretched.

Her scalp prickled. She felt hot and cold all at once, and her palm stung as though the toxic water had wet it. She could not rub or touch it for fear of disturbing Nara's rest, but soon it was throbbing like nettle-rash.

Here and there she caught flashes of Ogham on the felled trees, more 'all dead', or 'all fled', or else 'safe' scrawled through with thick lines and replaced with a warning. She imagined the slow, dawning horror of it, realising the wood that was your home and haven was turning on you.

But hadn't they begun it, with their quest to find the Anchorite? They had killed the trees, and so the trees were killing them. The words stayed on her lids when she closed them, mixing with images of the general and Sami, their faces turning swollen and milk-eyed as the dead fish.

The queen seemed not to notice the words written everywhere, speaking only to check with Ysolda they were on the right route or to urge the wolf faster on. She clearly did not speak Ogham, and this gave Ysolda a thrill of usefulness, to know something else this powerful woman did not.

The ground was at last beginning to change – felled alders broke the monotony of pine, mosses gave way to lichens that liked salty air. Nara woke and snapped her beak, tasting the sea. They were nearing the end of the vast forest already, an unimaginable distance swallowed by the panting wolves, driven on by Seren's determination and worse, her fear. Ysolda could sense it coming from the queen in waves. It was almost like a light was shining from her, red and angry and scribbled as the lines on the trees.

Ysolda shook her head to clear it, but it felt heavy on her neck. The queen's body was tense beneath Ysolda's hands, and her eyes scanned the surrounding trees every few seconds, as though waiting for men to emerge from the tangled roots.

They changed wolves again at dawn, and Seren did not even pull them to a complete stop, but leaped from one wolf to another and impatiently helped Ysolda across after her. She handed her some flatbread, but Ysolda's mouth was so dry she could barely swallow. She gave it to Nara instead, and gratefully accepted a last swallow of water before the queen urged the rested wolf forward through the thinning, uprooted trees.

CHAPTER TWENTY-NINE

FEVER

The treeline broke under a grey midday, the sun a pale yellow ghost behind clouds. Pine needles scattered compacted sand, and the wolf climbed a dune that had to lead to the beach. Ysolda barely registered the smell of salt, for her nostrils were filled with something else, something rotten and wrong, and her vision was blurry. Her hand now felt very hot, her eyelids heavy as skimming stones.

'The coast, at last,' said Seren joyfully. 'I never doubted you, Glaw Wood girl!'

But Ysolda had an awful feeling. Sickness, and something else, something the smell told her that her mind could not yet understand. It was like the trees, voiceless but etched with warning. Dread, of what lay over that dune. The wolf reached the top. There was the sea, and in it—

'My gods.' Seren pulled the wolf to a stop, the second halting beside them, panting. Ysolda followed her gaze, blinking to clear the blur.

Boats filled the natural cove before them. Large boats, interspersed with smaller, brightly painted vessels, bobbing on the strangely still water, smooth as Mirror Lake. Another blink, and Ysolda saw: these smaller shapes were not boats. They were people. Kaltis, painted in their blue and black, the dye leaching into the water around them where it lapped at their skin.

'The wood,' said Seren, almost to herself. 'This is what Boreal spoke of, the ones who tried to escape. The forest would not let them leave.'

Ysolda threw up a stale mouthful of water. Nara flew screeching into the air, and Ysolda overbalanced, falling from the wolf and landing hard on the sand, rolling over and over, her palm lancing with pain as she tumbled down the dune to rest in the lapping tide.

She wanted to run screaming, but her tongue and legs were lead. It was easier to lie here, float away. Her vision blurred again, and the world became vague shapes of unbearable brightness.

She closed her eyes, but now, painted over the Ogham words of warning, and dull-eyed Sami, and dead General Shivani were the tide of dead Kaltis, the men and women killed by the trees they had chopped to build their boats.

She was falling deeper into a nightmare, and she heard Seren's voice, but did not understand it. Another lancing pain in her hand, and she heard a sharp intake of breath.

'You're struck. Why did you not tell me you were shot?'

But Ysolda did not understand. She could see only terrible shapes and colours, hear roaring in her ears, and then a pain so awful it dragged her down and away, deep into unconsciousness.

A wrenching in her flesh.

A woman with teeth like a wolf biting her side.

A man with a metal beard and hair laughing, laughing.

She could hear screaming, and thought it was Sami. She reached for him, and was pushed away.

Hard talons kneaded her hair. She was made of feathers, and could fly.

The sun was bright and then it was midnight.

The Forgiver stepped from the dark mouth of a cave, her deer-skull headdress monstrously large. *You will lose the one you love three times.* She held a hag stone to her eye, and through it her pale blue iris became black as obsidian. Ysolda tipped forward, through the hole, and into the sky.

A girl was waiting in the stone.

And Hari was calling her back home.

Water trickled over her lips. She opened them and drank, though her throat felt swollen and raw. She heaved, but did not bring it up.

More water, and then an unfamiliar taste, tart and spicy and sour-sweet as early fruit. She swallowed, and opened her mouth for more. A woman chuckled.

'You like achaar,' said Seren. 'You have better taste than most, Glaw Wood girl.'

Ysolda opened her eyes. She was lying in the open, under a sky pitted with stars, her head on Seren's lap. The queen was spooning something into her mouth from a jar.

'What is it?'

'Pickled lime. The last of it.'

Ysolda swallowed again and struggled upright.

'Careful,' said Seren. 'You've been gone hours. Let the blood come back.'

'What happened?' said Ysolda, wincing as her hand flashed with pain.

'You were shot. A poisoned arrow, in your palm. It had

left flint behind. I had to remove it, but there was already some infection. Your hawk brought sea moss to soak away the blood, and I washed it with sura and stitched it.'

Ysolda looked down. 'Sura?'

'A strong spirit, from my first realm.'

Ysolda eyed her palm. It was a mass of stitches, the skin pink but no longer fiercely hot. Her head swam as Nara thudded down on her shoulder again and nuzzled into her hair.

'I am not a skilled seamstress.' The wolf queen smiled. 'But your fever has broken, and the wound was small. You will heal soon.'

Ysolda looked past her at the sea. The current had dispersed many of the bodies and boats, but a few remained. And just below the surface of the water, Ysolda thought she saw something solid – a piece of land nearly risen. A tidal path.

'I don't understand,' said Ysolda. 'What's happening? How can the trees change like this?'

Terror was growing in her chest. She wanted to be back in Glaw Wood, to know her home was still safe, but Seren was already getting to her feet, brushing sand from her fine clothes. Despite their treacherous and long journey, she still looked radiant and composed, her hair freshly washed in seawater and braided in a tight rope down her back.

'That is not for you to worry about. We must carry on.'

'What now?' said Ysolda, dazed.

'That is a question for my navigator,' said Seren. 'I hope you have not brought us to a dead end?'

CHAPTER THIRTY

CROSSING

Seren pointed at the horizon. Ysolda squinted, trying to ignore the floating bodies, but there was nothing to see except the sea and beyond it a fog, impenetrable as a cliff face. The tidal path was showing, but who knew where it led. If they took it and they did not find land before the tide turned, a current would sweep them out to sea.

Ysolda swallowed. She knew Seren would not hesitate to dispose of her if she thought she had led her astray. Her heart was thumping, and she pressed her hand to it. Her palm touched stone. She drew out from her tunic the hag stone Kore had given her, the one she'd bled on and Kore had told her to show the Anchorite.

'What is that?' Seren's eyes were narrowed. 'An adder stone, isn't it? Like the ones my Forgiver uses to read our fates.'

'Yes,' said Ysolda. There was no point denying it. 'She gave it to me, on the beach.'

'Why?' There was jealousy in Seren's voice.

'She said I needed it, to lead us safely.' A half-truth, better than the whole.

'Its talismanic power did not extend so far,' said Seren broodily, and Ysolda knew she was thinking of Ani, of Bala and Haddi, of Cai and the general. Maybe even of Sami.

Look through it on foggy days. It will clear the mists.

Ysolda held the stone up to her eye. For a moment, nothing but water and fog. And then . . .

In the far distance, a shape too large and solid to be a trick of a wave. Still distant, still dangerously far, but Ysolda could name it. An island, covered in trees. The End-World Wood.

'I see it,' she said, excitement making her voice shake. 'It's there.'

'Let me see,' said Seren hungrily. She snatched the hag stone from Ysolda's hand, nearly throttling her as she held it up to her own eye. 'Where?'

'There,' said Ysolda, pointing straight ahead. 'Past the fog.'

'I can see nothing past the fog.'

'Wait—'

'I have waited!' Seren was furious as she threw the hag

stone from her, the rock hitting Ysolda on the bridge of the nose. 'I see nothing!'

Eyes watering, Ysolda hastily held the hag stone back to her eye. She did not want to anger the queen further, but she could not deny the proof of her own eyes – the shape was there. The island lay in the fog.

'It is there, my queen,' she said soothingly. 'I swear it.'

'You had better be right.' There was clear bitterness in Seren's voice. She hated that Ysolda could see something she could not. She hated not being in control. For the first time, Ysolda felt a flush of power, of triumph. Kore's gift was special to her, meant only for her. In anyone else's hands, even the wolf queen's, it was a useless trinket.

'I swear it.'

'Then there is no time to waste. The tide will not wait, and the Anchorite has waited long enough. But if you are wrong . . .'

She let the sentence hang like a noose. Ysolda gulped.

Ysolda kept her gaze on the horizon, checking every so often through the hag stone that the island was definitely there, but still she could see the bodies in the edge of her vision as the wolf began its crossing.

She rode Ravi, and the power of the animal was clear through the reins. She knew she controlled him only by the queen's orders, but she felt something close to liking for the creature that had carried her so far and safely. Nara glided overhead, criss-crossing the rising sun as the wolves' feet left the sandy ground and found the newly revealed tidal causeway.

'You spoke of your sister, I think,' said Seren. Her eyes were fixed on the horizon fog, but her voice was curious. 'When you were in your fever. Hari, is it?'

'Yes,' said Ysolda, a hazy vision coming to her of Hari standing at their stone house's door, calling for her to come home.

'She is very gifted, a listener of trees.'

'Yes.'

'We heard of her, from traders. She has quite the reputation.' Seren cast her a sharp glance. 'But you are not gifted? That was not a lie?'

'No. I navigate, only.'

'For your sake, I hope you see what you say.'

There was silence a moment, only the faint splash of the wolves breaking a path through the shallow water.

'You will free her?' asked Ysolda. 'When we reach the End-World Wood?'

'When we find the Anchorite, yes.'

Ysolda felt a rush of misgiving.

'That's Shiv's knife, at your waist?'

Ysolda looked down. She had not remembered it was

there. She pulled the ornate knife from her belt and held it out to the queen. Seren leaned out over the water and took it, her hand cool and dry. 'A gift, upon the birth of her daughter, I believe.'

'Yes.'

'She told you?' Seren looked at Ysolda curiously. 'She seemed somewhat soft on you. Her family are at home. In the south of my first realm,' corrected the queen. 'Her daughter would be your age, perhaps. Shiv has been with me since the beginning. Twenty years, nine realms. But she knew it would be best to let her child settle somewhere. She sent her infant back, and Shiv chose to follow me.'

Suddenly, there were tears in Seren's eyes. It was as strange as watching a mountain cry. 'She was a fine warrior. A fine friend. A sister. Here—' Seren handed the knife back. 'She gave it to you. You should have it.'

'She wanted it back,' said Ysolda hesitantly.

'She has no need for it, now.' The queen changed the subject abruptly. 'When you met my daughter, what did she say?'

'Not much,' said Ysolda. 'She wanted to eat my hawk.'

Seren snorted. 'She is difficult, Eira. She always has been. She was born claiming the sky was the sea and vice versa. Nothing went unchallenged. But still, I did not see . . .' The queen frowned, her profile strong against the hazy sky. 'I did not see her betrayal coming.'

Ysolda wondered what this betrayal was. Running away? Seeking the Anchorite?

'What did she take from you?' asked Seren. 'She must have taken something. It is her way.'

The question caught Ysolda unawares. 'A necklace.'

'She's a habitual collector.'

Like you, thought Ysolda.

'She thinks she can lay claim to anything she likes.' Seren sighed. 'I did not teach her limits. I never planned to have a child, but Eira likes to ruin the best of plans.'

The queen's words were dismissive, even cold, but in her voice there was a begrudging pride for her thieving, difficult daughter.

'I got that impression,' said Ysolda.

'What is worst,' said Seren, and her voice was suddenly thick, 'is that I did not answer her questions completely. If I had, perhaps she would have understood how impossible it is for a child to do this alone. Perhaps she would have understood I do not do this for power, but to save all I hold dear. Including her. That is another thing I never told her enough.'

But Ysolda was not listening. She had sensed the change in the ground before she held the hag stone to her eye to confirm it.

She pulled hard on Ravi's ruff. 'Stop!'

She was only just in time.

CHAPTER THIRTY-ONE

BOG MOOR

Seren's reactions were like the touch of flame to dry straw, but still she was not fast enough. Tej moaned as his feet left the safety of the tidal path and sank flank deep into bog.

'What the—' Seren stood atop the wolf's back to save her feet from the sucking mud. 'I don't understand!'

She sounded as furious as she did fearful, and Ysolda could understand why. If it hadn't been for a lifetime of Glaw Wood bogs, Ysolda would not have noticed the smell, the slight blurring of the ground. But after her encounter with Eira, she would not be caught in a bog again. She had stopped Ravi at the very edge of the safe path and even then, the way ahead looked unchanged – a thin strip of seaweed-strewn land stretching into thick fog.

A glance through the hag stone showed otherwise. The bog became more defined, a vast uncovered expanse of black mud, bubbling in places where air sought to escape the depthless clutches of the molten dirt. It was no simple, small bog: it was vast, lying the extent of the remaining distance to the End-World Wood. A bog moor, easily a mile across, and the wolf queen and her wolf were stuck fast, sinking.

For a moment, a darker voice whispered in Ysolda's head, *Leave them.* Why should she help them? After all they'd done, not only to her and Hari but Uncle, Aunty, Sami and the Forgiver. All those people, taken from their homes, and who knows how many others stolen or killed in Seren's quest for power.

But even as the thought rose, it popped like an air bubble. Ysolda could not act in such a cold-hearted way – and leaving the queen would mean leaving Tej too. The wolf's hind legs were swallowed now, and he was looking around with wide, white-edged eyes.

'Lie flat,' said Ysolda. 'Spread your weight along his back.'

Seren lay on her belly, arms wrapped around Tej's neck.

'There's a more solid patch to your right. He needs to swim to it.'

'I can't see it—'

'It's there,' said Ysolda, squinting through the hag stone.

A thin thread of safe ground spread out ahead, woven between the sucking mud all the way to the island. It was marked by the slightest dryness of the ground, a lighter colour, and she could only see it through the hag stone. But it was there, as sure as the island itself.

'It's not far, an arm's length away. When you get close, you can jump from his back and help pull him out.'

But Seren was shaking her head. Without seeing safety with her own eyes, she would not believe it.

Ysolda chewed her tongue in irritation. 'I'll show you.'

She whistled and jerked her head at the patch of ground. Nara took off at once and swooped low over Tej's head, landing a foot away on the solid ground.

'She is lighter than us,' snapped the queen. 'How do I know this safe place, if it exists, will support us?'

There was nothing for it. Ysolda took another tight grip of Ravi's ruff. 'Listen, wolf,' she said firmly. 'We need to save your friend and your queen. So I need you to take a run-up and jump to where my hawk is, all right?'

Ravi didn't move.

'Please,' said Ysolda, almost shouting in frustration. 'Tell him to listen to me.'

'Ravi,' said the queen. 'Obey.'

Ysolda repeated her request, and the wolf growled, but did as he was bid. He stepped back a few feet and then leaped, lightly and easily, over Tej's head. They landed on the solid ground, scattering Nara, and Ysolda turned to look at Seren.

'Now,' she said. 'You don't have much time. Make him swim forward.'

Seren did not waste another moment. She leaned close to her wolf's ear and whispered. Tej obeyed, though his eyes were still rolling in fear. The progress was agonising, each movement causing him to sink faster, but within two strokes the queen was able to leap from his back on to the safe ground beside Ysolda.

Ysolda slid ungracefully from Ravi's back to stand beside the queen. She half-expected Seren to suggest they continued, being so close to their goal, but her eyes were fixed on her wolf. She seemed to truly love the creatures, more even than the general, or her own daughter.

'Now what?' the wolf queen asked.

'We will have to pull him. And quickly.' Ysolda eyed Tej's tail, the tip only just visible. 'Tell him not to move, but if he could grip on to something—'

'Ravi.' The queen clicked her fingers, and the wolf walked forward. She removed her copper-threaded shawl and placed one end in Ravi's mouth. 'Tej.' He opened his mouth, and she placed the other end into his. Then she kneeled and used the end of her spear to dig two small holes into the ground. Into these she placed her heels, braced to pull on Tej's front leg. Ysolda copied her.

'On three,' said Seren, in control once more. '*Ek, do, teen* – pull!'

The three of them pulled. For a moment it felt like the bog's hold was too strong, but then the queen counted to three in her first realm's language again – *ek, do, teen!* – and Tej began to move. Ysolda's shoulders screamed, the muscles straining, but on the final count the bog released its grip with an immense sucking sound, like a whirlpool in reverse.

'Yes!' she shouted as Tej bounded free, whining plaintively, and Ravi dropped the copper shawl to the ground and began licking the mud from his companion's flank.

The queen did not bother to retrieve her precious shawl, only wrapped her arms around Tej's neck and whispered into his ear until he stopped whining. Ysolda massaged her arms, and Nara landed once more on her shoulder. She stroked the hawk while Seren soothed her wolf, and felt she understood the queen for the very first time.

After a few minutes, Seren turned back to Ysolda, eyes bright. She looked as though she were about to thank her, but instead she mounted Tej. 'Well then. We should go. After you.'

Ysolda led the way in silence. With the hag stone at her eye she could see the safe ground, without it they were soon enshrined in fog. But when she looked back, the way behind was obvious, clear. It was as though by walking it, they were making it real, revealing it to the naked eye.

'Strange,' said Seren, following Ysolda's gaze. 'But at least it will make our route back easier. Did the Forgiver tell you anything of this?'

'No,' said Ysolda. 'She only gave me the hag stone.'

Seren made a chewing motion, like she was biting back unsaid words. Then, taking Ysolda by surprise she asked, 'Where are your parents?'

'Dead.'

'I see. Mine too. When I was younger than Eira. She does not know how lucky she is. Or was? Maybe. Maybe she is still out there somewhere. She studied enough maps to know what routes were once safe. But as Boreal said, it is all changing.' The queen looked behind them again, towards the now far-off shore.

Ysolda looked too. There was no sign of Boreal or his men, and at this distance, she could no longer make out the terrible shapes in the water.

'It's clear Boreal does not know of this island's existence,' said Seren, and Ysolda noticed with relief that Seren had decided to trust what Ysolda could see through the hag stone. 'Or else he would have felled it, too.'

'Yes,' said Ysolda, her disgust at the destruction clear in her voice.

Seren's tone hardened. 'You think us possessed, to travel so far, destroy so much?'

This was exactly what she was thinking. 'No.'

'This is beyond your understanding, Glaw Wood girl. Beyond many people's understanding.'

There was nothing to say to that. The island drew closer and closer, Tej close behind Ravi as they leaped from safe spot to safe spot, leaving behind pawprints showing the secure route. The smell of mud and salt was strong in Ysolda's nostrils, and the wind was starting to pick up, sending sea spray into her face and chilling her hands.

Soon they were close enough for Ysolda to see the details of the End-World Wood – the curved canopies of alder and elm and oak and birch, familiar to Ysolda from home. Watching the ancient wood approach, for the first time in a long time Ysolda allowed herself to feel excitement.

All her childhood the Glaw Wood dwellers had spoken and been proud of their link to this ancient patch, the last of the first forest planted by the Anchorite that once had carpeted the Isles, the place where all other trees were seeded from. And here was the last piece of it, saved by sea and having fallen out of stories. The last piece, other than their Elder Alder. A link, stretching back through millennia, and more importantly for Ysolda, back to her home on the other edge of the Isles.

Could it be that this place housed an ancient girl, old as

the trees she lived in? Perhaps it was spending so much time with Lakes people, perhaps it was all she had seen and done, but as the trees loomed above them and their famous roots arched like gnarled ceilings tall enough to walk through, Ysolda thought, for the first time, *Maybe*.

CHAPTER THIRTY-TWO

THE END-WORLD WOOD

The moment the wolves' paws touched the sandy shore, Ysolda heard Seren gasp. She dropped the hag stone from her eye, and saw why. The island had materialised, solid and fogless, real even without the hag stone's clarifying gaze.

'You were right, Glaw Wood girl,' said Seren. 'It really is here.'

It is, thought Ysolda, *and so are we.*

The wind grew stronger as the wolves scrambled up a tightly shelving beach of loose sand twined through the thick roots. These roots must once have sat in the earth, but time and wind and sea had licked them clean, exposing them like mighty skeletons, and the trunks had grown on regardless, reaching for the fast-running clouds.

Ysolda had never seen such huge trees. They barely even swayed in the wind ripping through them. They grew higher than Seren's castle, higher than the tallest-masted ship Ysolda had ever seen. As high, it felt, as the wolves approached their branches' shelter, as the sky. The trunks were too wide to encompass in her arms, even the birches', which usually grew slimmer.

Every branch was in full leaf, their foliage glossy green, though Glaw Wood's would surely be yellow and brown by now and being strewn by the inhabitants with gifts and ribbons for the festival of Mabon. These trees did not grow with the same instincts as others Ysolda had seen, avoiding one another's space, keeping roots and crowns apart to avoid injury or infection. These branches grew into and around one another, twining like vines, and their roots did the same. Ysolda felt a rush of homesickness, and her eyes prickled with wind and wanting as Ravi reached the boundary to the End-World Wood and sank down, panting.

The queen dismounted Tej and approached the nearest roots as tentative as Ysolda had ever seen her. 'Like banyans,' she said, voice snatched at by the growing gale. 'Trees from my first realm. The roots grow up and out of the ground like this. But they grow from other trees. These are growing together, not against each other.' Her voice was full of wonder. 'I have never seen anything like it.'

'Nor I,' croaked Ysolda, sliding off Ravi as Nara landed once more on her shoulder.

'Well, Glaw Wood girl,' said the queen, peering into the darkness beneath the roots, 'you've brought us this far. Now to find the Anchorite.'

The queen returned to Tej and opened the pack strapped to his ruff. She pulled out a lighting flint and a short, thick blade. As she approached the trees once more, her thick braid flying, Ysolda realised that she intended to cut some wood from the End-World Wood to light as a torch.

'No!' Ysolda acted on instinct, stepping in front of the blade even as the queen raised it. 'My queen, this place is sacred. The Anchorite would not think us good guests if we arrived with a hacked-off piece of her home.'

The queen was still paused in the act of the swing, and with the blade raised over her head she looked fearsome. But after a moment's thought she lowered it, nodding agreement. 'Find me some fallen wood.'

Ysolda scanned the steep beach. There was some driftwood, lifted high enough from the tideline to be dry to the touch. She collected a few gnarled pieces, head bowed against the fierce air, and returned to Seren. As the queen bound them together, Ysolda gathered some moss that grew on the massive roots, thanking the trees silently for providing.

'What's that for?' asked Seren.

'In this wind it will be hard to light. That spirit you have,' said Ysolda, 'it sounds like life water. It's a spirit the traders sometimes bring from the continent.'

'Life water.' The queen smiled. 'I've heard of it. Suna is a finer spirit – softer, sweeter.'

'Well, once, Gwen and Gwyn had too much life water, and they knocked over a candle near their flagons. There was only the scarcest drop left, but it was enough to set their table alight. Since then, they swore off it for drinking, but use it as firelighter when the wood is wet or scarce.'

Seren laughed, a light, clear sound snatched away by the breeze, which caught Ysolda by surprise. 'Glaw Wood resourcefulness. I've heard tell of it. I should like to meet this Gwen and Gwyn.'

Ysolda was certain it would not be mutual. The queen's good spirits made her uneasy. She was certain they had reached the end of her quest, a mission that had seen Thane Boreal destroy his own forest and the queen sacrifice many lives for. But as Ysolda watched the woman merrily soaking the moss in suna, she was far from certain they'd find what they were looking for – either of them. There was no sign of a boat, no evidence that Eira was on the island. If they failed to find the amulet and the Anchorite both, what then?

The queen struck the flint, and a spark leaped into the

suna-soaked moss. It caught instantly and she deftly stuck it into the bunch of driftwood, the whole thing blazing bright and smokeless, buffeted by the wind.

'She lives at the heart, yes?' said the queen, and because that is where the story said the Anchorite lived and Ysolda had no other ideas, she nodded. Seren walked to her wolves, who had flopped by the steep beach. She pressed her forehead to each muzzle. 'Rest here, Tej, Ravi. Stay sheltered. You did well, but it may become narrow further on. At any sign of a boat, call for me.'

Tej sighed in answer, and Ravi rested his huge head on his paws, eyebrows twitching. Seren squared her shoulders, lifted the torch high, and stepped into the tunnelled roots. They dwarfed her, the light dissolving before it struck the underside of the cavern. Before Ysolda followed, she turned to Nara.

'I'll need you to lead us, Nara. Stay close to the roots, show us to the middle.'

The hawk snipped her beak in understanding and took off to alight on the cavernous roots over the waiting queen's head. Sending up a silent prayer to the ancient trees, Ysolda stepped once more into the unknown.

The torch was essential – the roots were so tightly knotted they let in scant light. Only the wind found its way in, whistling through the gaps and setting up a haunting whine.

If the passageways had not been so spacious, Ysolda might have felt stifled, but even a horse could have passed through. The floor was a mix of sand and soil, the smell salty and full of darkness. It reminded Ysolda of the sea caves where Hari was kept, and she wished her sister was with her. *But if she were, you would not have to be here, walking this place with the wolf queen*, she reminded herself.

Their entry point led them straight a long time, and they walked in silence, listening to the howling wind, eventually reaching a gnarl of criss-crossed routes, spinning away in every direction. Ysolda searched for Nara's shadow through the far-off roots, and found it. The hawk was wheeling over the tunnel that, she guessed, would take them to the centre of the island.

'This way,' she pointed, and Seren nodded, following. The torch cast her beautiful face into harsh shadows, the whites of her eyes glinting like teeth. Ysolda shuddered as she turned away. She had no plan, no idea what she would do when they reached the heart of the island. If the Anchorite was not there, would Seren blame her?

And if she is there, said a smaller, but determined voice, *you have led the wolf queen to her. What will she do to the ancient girl?*

Ysolda pushed the thought from her mind. The Anchorite did not exist, and whatever came, Ysolda could not change that.

They moved deeper into the root tunnels, which narrowed as the queen had predicted, but were still more than high enough for humans. Every few minutes Ysolda searched the high arcs for Nara's shadow. Once or twice she thought she'd lost the hawk, or the hawk had lost them, but then a shape would briefly plumb the gaps of light. At every crossroads, Nara would mark the way by flying back and forth until Ysolda whistled her understanding, the hawk somehow hearing her over the wind.

'You are a good team,' remarked the queen, when they had been walking perhaps an hour. 'You had her since an eyas?'

'Yes,' said Ysolda. 'A storm killed her parents. I found her tumbled on the beach. My sister said it was too late to train her, but I couldn't leave her.'

'Everyone said I could not train a wolf,' said Seren. 'But they did not understand how determined I was. Tej's grandmother was the first. I took her from the coast of the Thawless Circle, a place far west of these isles where wolves can swim as well as otters. She was a pup, and though she bit me, I forgave her. She bit me again, and I forgave her again. I met her bites with kisses. I taught her my love was better than my anger. All my wolves are raised to know this.'

Ysolda looked sideways at the queen. So there was no magic that bound her to the wolves. Ysolda supposed she should not be surprised – Seren did not have wolf's teeth, or eat raw meat like in the stories. Nor, according to the torch burning in her hand, could she see in the dark. But still, it was strange to know the wolf queen was a woman with a knack for training wolves, not some supernatural beast. She was like Ysolda and her hawk.

Nara let out a screech from somewhere a little ahead, muted by the wind but still audible. Ysolda's heart raced at the sudden sound, but it was not her warning cry. It was a caw of triumph. She looked ahead, where the ground sloped gently away before them. And there, carved into a root over the slope, was a marking Ysolda could read only too well.

Home.

CHAPTER THIRTY-THREE

THE ANCHORITE'S NEST

Ysolda felt numb. Until she had seen that marking, it was easy to dismiss the occasional thought about the Anchorite somehow existing in these mighty roots. The whole island felt untouched by human influence – no breaks in the trees, no smells of cooking or signs of wells drilled into the dirt. No animals that could keep a person alive, even a person of myth and matchless age.

Because surely, *surely*, if the ancient girl was real, the people of Glaw Wood would have known. The fact would not have faded into myth and then into folktale, told to entertain small children by the fire, or else laugh at those who believed such a thing not only possible, but true.

There were so many versions of the story. The Anchorite

was a girl who swore an oath of silence and solitude in order to be told the secrets of the world. The Anchorite was a girl who traded her heart for the ability to grow forests, and planted Glaw Wood. The Anchorite was a girl who wished to become a tree and so walled herself up inside one. The Anchorite was a story, just a story.

But there on the root over their heads was the evidence of a person, the writing sure and neat. A human hand had pressed those markings into the wood. A person who called this place home.

Ysolda felt the world as she knew it crumbling beneath her.

'What does that say?' asked the queen, her voice hungry.

'Home.'

'She is here,' breathed Seren, and in her tone Ysolda heard disbelief. So even the wolf queen had come all this way without certainty. 'We found her.'

Ysolda allowed herself to feel glad. This meant Hari would be freed. The general had told her Seren was a woman of her word, and Ysolda longed to believe her. She clutched the slain warrior's knife in her belt and whistled to Nara, to tell her they'd found the place they sought. The hawk gave no reply, probably perched in the branches high above their heads, preening herself with pride.

Seren topped up the moss with trembling fingers, making the flame burn stronger. They ducked under the inscribed root, and the queen held the torch higher to light the cavern.

Of all the sights Ysolda had seen, from the queen's castle to Mirror Lake, this was the most humbling. It was like a massive hall of trees, the tangled roots arching out in an intricate pattern over the deeply hollowed ground. It looked like a cooking bowl with a beautifully carved lid. At the centre of the hollow's roof was the underside of a tree that dwarfed all others. Ravi and Tej could have lain nose to tail and not reached its width. Some of its roots dropped straight down to pool on the floor like ropes, and despite the size Ysolda recognised it as an alder. It was like being in the presence of a god.

They moved down the slope, the queen no longer walking ahead but side by side with Ysolda, whose head was spinning as she looked at the ceiling of roots above her. It was not as random as she'd first thought, the patterns more like a spider's web, a structure secure and perfect. It was darker here, the gaps filled with earth, and the wind did not reach them. The only sounds were their footsteps muffled on the sandy soil, the crackle of the burning torch.

They seemed in unspoken agreement about where they were heading. There was nowhere else to go. The entire space, the entire island, the entire journey had led them here, and was arrowing them towards the massive tree with its hanging roots. They reached the underside of the trunk and peered up into its shadowy mass. Far, far above them, was a pinprick of light.

'The trunk,' Ysolda breathed. 'It's hollow.'

The queen nodded, seemingly speechless. She approached the dangling roots and held the torch close to inspect them. They were notched, the marks made so long ago the tree had healed around them, bulges grown over the scored streaks. But it was clear someone, long ago, had used them as a ladder to access the trunk.

'Well,' said Seren, in a quiet voice. 'After you.'

Ysolda blinked stupidly at her.

Seren raised her eyebrow. 'The navigator should surely go first.'

Ysolda swallowed, craning her neck. The pinprick of light was very far away. She was a skilled tree climber of course, every Glaw Wood dweller was, and the roots were thick as a trunk. But they stretched higher than anything she had scaled before, and Ysolda was tired, legs weak from days on wolfback, her palm still smarting from the stitches. She felt a firm hand on her back, pushing her forward. Seren was not going to give her a choice.

And didn't a part of Ysolda, a large and loud part, want to see what lay in that old and hollow trunk?

She moved the knife around to her back so it would not impede her climbing. The stitches pulled as she reached up to the first notch, the blistered wood offering grip.

Wrapping her legs around the root, she began to climb, hand over hand, her legs locked tight at the ankle. She let her breath pace her movements, and slowly her heart stopped pounding.

She had just settled into a rhythm when she heard a noise below her. The queen had set the torch in the sandy ground and had begun her ascent on an adjacent root. She was strong but obviously unused to climbing trees, and her technique was not as neat as Ysolda's.

The climb was even further than it had looked from the ground. Just as reaching the island had meant crossing a deceptive distance, the trunk seemed to tunnel away from her. As long as she focused on one hand, then the other, legs following after, she knew she could do it, but the moment she looked up or down it felt impossible.

She wondered if the Anchorite had come here before the roots had been exposed. The notches marking the roots suggested someone had needed to move to and from the tree since the ground had retreated, but all the stories said that when the Anchorite left the End-World Wood, its death was not long behind. Ysolda noticed vaguely she had stopped tempering her musings about the ancient girl with *ifs*. The closer she drew to the trunk, the more certain she was they were approaching the Anchorite's nest.

Finally, she hauled herself into the base of the hollow trunk, where the roots created a sort of woven floor. She felt her way to the edge, where the matting was thickest, and waited inside the dark silence for the queen to catch up. At last Seren pulled herself on to the platform, and picked her way to Ysolda.

Slowly, their eyes adjusted to the dark. The space they now stood in was large as Ysolda's house across, and all around them were signs of habitation. Hooks lined the walls, and a tangle of sheets was huddled against the opposite side of the trunk. Ysolda's breath hitched as she thought she saw them stir, but it was only a shadow, perhaps Nara, from high above.

'Anchorite?' said Seren, searching the dimness. 'Anchorite, are you there?'

Ysolda edged around the side of the hollow trunk, towards the pile of sheets. Another flicker from high above them stopped her in her tracks, but it moved on once more. At last she reached them, a mix of patchworked furs and worn wool. They were bundled tightly, piled, and smelling of must and abandonment.

Holding her breath, Ysolda reached out. Her fingers were pale in the gloom and again she thought she saw movement in the fabric. What would she look like, this ancient girl? Would it be just a skeleton? Her hand trembled, but Ysolda gritted her teeth and pulled the top sheet back.

Her heart sank. There was no one there. Not even the dust of long-lying bones.

'Not there,' said Ysolda to herself, and then, louder, 'Not here.'

'What?' called Seren.

'She's not here!' shouted Ysolda, her voice echoing. 'The Anchorite. She's gone.'

'Gone, is she?' said a deep, familiar voice.

Ysolda froze in horror. Seren's eyes glinted from the opposite edge of the trunk. Ysolda peered through the latticework of roots. Far below them, and unmistakable, stood flame-haired Thane Boreal.

CHAPTER THIRTY-FOUR

BETRAYED

Stay there, mouthed Seren. Ysolda nodded her understanding. How had they not heard the wolves howl? But then, the wind had been so strong, perhaps it had swallowed their warning.

'We know you are up there,' said Thane Boreal, almost lazily. 'Nice of you to show the path across the bog moor, though we lost a few.' He did not seem concerned.

Ysolda looked down again. He was surrounded by ten Kaltis, including Elgin, their bows drawn and arrows trained up into the trunk. And there – Ysolda's heart leaped – was Sami beside him, arm in a sling, face bruised, muddy and miserable. But then it dawned on her – he had led them here. He had joined Thane Boreal and betrayed them.

The thane was smiling, his strong yellow teeth illuminated

by their abandoned torch, bright against his dyed lips. 'I'm afraid if you do not have the Anchorite, there is little point keeping you alive.' He raised his hand, and the archers pulled back their arms.

'We do!' shouted Ysolda. 'She's here!'

'That you, Glaw Wood girl?' said Thane Boreal. 'We just heard you. You said she's—'

'Gone, yes,' called Ysolda, feeling Seren's eyes burn into her. 'Passed out. I thought she was dead, but she's breathing!'

It was a thin story, but looking at Boreal's face she could see the desperation there, the hunger for her words to be true.

'Show me,' he said.

'I dare not move her. I fear she could crumble into dust.'

'What does she look like?' said the thane.

'Small as a doll,' said Ysolda, closing her eyes and letting her imagination fly. 'Her eyelids are closed and thin as shells. Her hair is long and dark and wraps her many times, like a cocoon. Her skin is grey as stone, her fingernails are like lengths of bark. She is dressed in ferns and moss, and she breathes, but only just.'

She opened her eyes. The queen was watching her with an odd expression on her face, and Ysolda's fists curled with the lie. Boreal was having a muffled conversation with Elgin.

Elgin nodded and shoved Sami forward. He spoke

harshly to the boy, who shook his head violently, gesturing to his sling. But Elgin ripped the bandage off, and Sami cried out in pain. Even at this distance, Ysolda could see his forearm was bruised yellow and black from where the wolf had trampled him. But as Sami flexed his fingers, it was clear it wasn't broken.

'We are sending a friend to find out,' said Thane Boreal, smirking. 'Scuttle along, little Lakes spider.'

It was brutal, watching Sami climb. He wrapped his injured elbow around the root and used his good arm to haul himself, his legs bent and bare feet braced against the wood for grip. He looked terrified but determined, and as he climbed higher the Kaltis stopped jeering and started up calls of encouragement.

'Come on, Sami,' murmured Ysolda. He passed the point where a fall would be survivable. As he got closer to the root platform, Ysolda edged forward and lay down on her belly, and as soon as his good hand gripped the roots, she took hold of his wrist and pulled with all her might. He collapsed down, panting, beside her. Seren had not moved from her position by the trunk.

'Well, boy?' called Thane Boreal. 'Do you see her?'

Sami and Ysolda turned their heads to face each other.

'She's not here, is she?' hissed Sami.

Defensiveness flared in Ysolda. 'You led them here!'

Sami's eyes narrowed. 'You left me.'

'Boy!' shouted Boreal. 'Is she there or not?'

'I have to tell him the truth,' said Sami.

'No, you don't.'

'They could have killed me, and they didn't. I owe them.'

'Please.' Ysolda grabbed for his hand, and accidentally knocked his sore wrist. Sami scowled and pushed himself upright. He caught sight of Seren. In that moment, seeing the hatred on his face, Ysolda knew all was lost.

'She lied,' called Sami. 'The Anchorite isn't here.'

'So be it,' said Thane Boreal, disappointment twisting his voice. 'Our quest continues, Raani. Or at least, mine does.'

'Don't do anything hasty, Boreal,' called Seren. 'There is still time to be allies yet—'

'I think I'm better off without allies like you,' said the thane. 'After I've searched what's left of my forest, I'll try Glaw Wood. I'll fell every tree if I have to.'

Dread bit into Ysolda's heart, spreading like snake venom until her limbs felt heavy as they had in her fever. Not Glaw Wood uprooted. Not her green and cherished home, reduced to dead timber by Boreal's fruitless quest.

'She's not there,' she shouted, her throat raw with fear. 'She doesn't exist! You're mad, both of you! She's not there, she's not in Glaw Wood. She's nowhere!'

'One way to find out.' There was a hateful pleasure in Thane Boreal's voice.

'Burn them all.'

'Wait,' said Sami, dangling his legs over the gap, preparing to slide down. 'Wait for me!'

An arrow flew past him in answer, missing by a whisker's width. Ysolda pulled him clear, right up to the thicker roots at the edge, where someone had once lain in a pile of blankets.

There was a moment's pause, before the unmistakable crackle of a flame catching rose up the hollow trunk. Ysolda peered once more through the latticework. Boreal had used their own torch to set the root aflame, and it was rising steadily, hungrily, travelling the makeshift ladder faster than any human could climb.

More arrows shot through the gaps in the floor, embedding above their heads or else falling in harmless loops to their feet. But Ysolda knew it was too late – the fire was already eating up their only means of escape.

She could only watch as Boreal ordered his men from the cavern, which was filling with smoke. Surely what he said had only been a cruel, final jibe. Surely he would not really go to Glaw Wood and destroy every tree?

More smoke floated up through the floor, catching in Ysolda's throat.

'What do we do?' Sami coughed, using his sleeve to filter out the smoke.

Ysolda rounded on him. 'You betrayed us. And for

what? So you could be left to die too?'

'Not now, children.' Seren was searching the trunk's inner walls. 'We have to climb. Quickly.'

Sami groaned, and Ysolda felt a hint of sympathy for the injured boy. 'Here,' she said, collecting up a few of the fallen arrows, 'use the flints as handholds.'

She showed him what she meant, protecting her hand with her sleeve and using the sharp points of the flint to hack into the wood and find purchase. From far below the pinprick of light had seemed singular, but now Ysolda saw it was diffuse, running from various seams in the trunk where the branches had cracked away. The nearest exit was closer than the ground had been.

'We can do this,' she urged Sami. 'Come on.'

She followed close behind him, occasionally supporting his weight on her shoulder. They were barely six feet off the ground when Ysolda felt a strong hand close on her ankle. She looked down. The Anchorite's nest was full of smoke. Spluttering, Seren had abandoned her attempt to escape up the opposite side, and now was pulling on Ysolda's ankles, scrabbling for the flints.

Ysolda cried out and tried to kick her off, but the wolf queen was too strong. Her grip faltered and then she was falling, into the gathering smoke.

CHAPTER THIRTY-FIVE

FURNACE

Bright stars exploded in front of Ysolda's eyes. The breath was doubly knocked from her by her landing on the roots, and by Sami landing hard atop her. Without her support, he had crumbled.

Smoke soon obscured Ysolda's vision and her lungs both, and she lay choking, eyes streaming, feeling heat, far off at first, on her back. Then it was licking her neck like a fiery tongue, and she knew she must move, must get up, must attempt the climb if she were to have any chance of surviving the growing inferno.

But it was easier, much easier, to lie there. She felt Sami's good hand in hers as he tried to haul her to her feet, heard him, through the growing roar of the fire, calling her name, telling her to 'Get up! *GET UP!*' but the flames were louder now, and sweat slickened their palms, made it hard for him to grip.

The queen was out of sight now. In Ysolda's increasingly clouded mind, thoughts swam up to meet her like the dead-eyed fish in the poison stream. *Of course the queen left me to die. If Glaw Wood is going, I want to be gone. The Anchorite was here, she exists – existed.*

And then, there she was. A grey-skinned, wide-eyed girl, looking down at her through the thickening smoke. Ysolda felt a jolt in her chest, and realised the Anchorite was hitting her.

'Come *on*, you stupid girl!'

Dimly, Ysolda registered that this wasn't very Anchorite-like language. Sweat slicked the girl's face, and through the trickle Ysolda saw her face was brown, and her eyes were a very familiar shade of amber.

'You,' choked Ysolda, batting Eira away. 'Thief.'

But Eira was stronger than Sami, and she had experience pulling Ysolda from danger. As she yanked Ysolda clear of the smoke, Ysolda felt her lungs open again, her mind slowly clearing. Her moment of weakness vanished in a rush of anger, and she shook Eira off her.

The roots beneath her were smoking. Not aflame yet, but the cavern below was obscured and at the centre of the trunk the ladder roots were a furnace, fast spreading towards them.

'This way!' Eira was motioning to a place where the darkness had been thickest, but now, with the firelight licking every inch of the trunk, Ysolda saw an overlap in the remaining sapwood, invisible from every angle but one. She pushed past Eira and pulled Sami towards it, coughing.

The crack was large enough only for a child, and Ysolda felt the wood change from sapwood to bark, the rough outer surface scraping as she edged through. A waft of fresh air hit her face as Sami tumbled after her, and the three of them collapsed on to the ground, coughing and heaving.

Instantly, Nara's soft feather cuffed her cheek as the hawk flew in panicked circles around her, checking for injury.

'It's all right, Nara,' she gasped. 'I'm all right.'

They were in the nook where exposed root met trunk, raised high from the ground. Smoke was seeping through, making it look like they sat in mist, and the heat was fierce even here. There was no sign of Thane Boreal, nor Seren. Only the trees of End-World Wood, vast and otherworldly, surrounded them. Eira was taking deep slurps of air, and Ysolda kicked out at her.

'My amulet,' she hissed. 'Where is it?'

'We have bigger problems,' said Eira. The first spurt of flame flickered through the gap they had just squeezed through. Sami yelped and backed further away.

'Quickly!' Eira shuffled to the edge of the roots, where

they dipped in a gentle slope towards the sandy dirt. 'This way.'

She slid down the wood, and Ysolda followed fast behind, Nara lifting off from her shoulder to swoop overhead. More smoke was rising behind them, at the far edge of the forest. Thane Boreal must have set more fires. Tears of fury prickled in Ysolda's eyes at the viciousness of it, the waste. This ancient wood, which had long stood and grown strong and seeded all other trees from it, was being destroyed, and for what? Boreal was a brute. Glaw Wood, *her* Glaw Wood, really was in danger.

They reached the ground, and Eira began to run. She was fast, and clearly better rested than Ysolda and Sami. How long had she been here on the island? She seemed to know exactly where she was going.

'What if it's a trap?' panted Sami. There was a small chance Eira was leading them to the wolf queen, but after everything Ysolda had gleaned from her time with Seren, she thought it was unlikely. Besides, she didn't see what choice they had.

'Slow down,' she shouted.

Eira dropped her pace, rolling her eyes at them over her shoulder. 'You do know the island is on fire?' she shouted. 'Speed up.'

Lungs burning, legs aching, side stinging, Ysolda gritted her teeth and tried to keep stride. Sami was smaller and more injured, but she tugged him alongside her, the rising sound of the fire chasing them through the trees. Ysolda was so intent on reaching the clear sky ahead, she did not watch her feet.

Her legs windmilled a moment, touching only air, and then she landed, hard, on the raked beach that edged the island. Pebbles struck her face and scraped her hands, and she dug in her fingers to stop herself sliding into the sea.

'Elegant as ever,' said Eira smugly. 'Nice cloak, by the way. We match.'

Still panting into the pebbles, Ysolda wheezed, 'Difference is, I didn't steal mine.'

'Ysolda,' mewled Sami. She looked up, face glowing, body breathless, and saw Eira standing calm and smirking, her hand raised and resting on a wolf's shoulder. Ravi's shoulder.

Sami whimpered, and Ysolda pushed herself to her feet, fumbling for the general's knife in her belt. She held it out before her, pushing Sami behind her, and scanning the beach for the wolf queen. But Seren was nowhere to be seen.

'Calm down,' said Eira, unconcerned. 'Is that Shiv's knife?'

'What are you doing?' snapped Ysolda.

'Saving your life, like always.'

'What about him,' said Ysolda, gesturing at Ravi. 'Where's your mother?'

'You know who I am?'

'Yes. And she likes you about as much as I do.'

'I saw you arrive together,' said Eira, a shadow crossing her face, 'but I didn't know you would swallow her poison.'

'Why do you have Ravi?'

'He's my favourite,' she said. 'And Tej would never have left the beach when my mother told him to stay.' She patted Ravi's muzzle. 'I thought he could be useful.'

'Useful for what?'

'For whatever comes next.' Her eyes slid past Ysolda to the forest behind. 'And more immediately, for getting us all off the island.'

Ysolda followed her gaze. Smoke was now billowing through the trunks bordering the beach. Sami whimpered and drew closer to her.

'Where's my amulet?'

'Calm down,' said Eira. 'I have it safe. I thought it was a key of some sort, but it's just a lump of sap.'

'It's amber.'

Eira shrugged. 'Old sap.'

'How did you get here?'

'Not very observant, are you?' Eira pointed. A small boat, more of a canoe, formed from a hollowed-out trunk of pine was camouflaged further along the beach, pebbles stacked high around it. 'Ravi can tow it,' she said. 'Now, quickly, the fire's getting closer.'

'We can't go back to shore,' said Sami, panicked. 'Boreal's men will be keeping watch.'

'And your mother is somewhere,' said Ysolda.

'She's long gone. She and Tej will be halfway to the mainland by now. We aren't going that way, anyway.'

'Which way are we going then?' asked Ysolda, exasperated.

Eira pulled something from her pocket and held it out to her. 'I was hoping you could tell me.'

CHAPTER THIRTY-SIX

HIGH PLACE

Ysolda took the object. It was a stick of alder wood, whittled with markings.

'You, boy,' said Eira. 'Help me tie the boat.'

They secured the pine dugout to Ravi with ropes from his saddlebag, then Eira climbed atop the wolf. Ysolda whistled Nara on to her shoulder as she studied the Ogham stick.

'You ride with me,' said the wolf queen's daughter to Ysolda. 'The boy can go in the boat.'

'You won't cut the ropes?' asked Sami, lip trembling.

Eira rolled her eyes. 'Not unless you really deserve it.'

'Of course we won't,' said Ysolda, briefly squeezing his good shoulder. Despite his betrayal, she felt fondly for the boy – at least, more fondly than she did towards Eira.

The approaching fire prevented further conversation. Ravi dragged the boat into shallow water, and Ysolda helped Sami inside, covering him with her cloak to keep him warm before clambering up behind Eira.

'Sweet,' said Eira. 'He your brother?'

'No.'

'Boyfriend?'

'No!'

'All right.' Eira grinned and ordered Ravi on. She had clearly learned her mother's knack for wolves. 'So, where we headed?'

'Where did you get this?' said Ysolda, waving the Ogham stick in Eira's periphery.

'What does it say?'

'I asked you first.'

Eira sighed. 'Fine. You know, I'd have hoped you'd have mellowed a bit, Glaw Wood girl. I found it in the Anchorite's nest. It was wrapped in her sheets, like a token.'

'So she was already gone when you arrived?'

'Obviously,' said Eira. 'Or else I wouldn't have hung around, would I? And you'd be crisping up nicely in that old tree.'

Ysolda shuddered and turned back to the island. It was truly ablaze now, and the sight made her chest ache. 'How did you get across the bog moor?'

'What do you mean?'

'The bog,' said Ysolda impatiently. 'How did you see it? Did you have a hag stone?'

'A what?'

'An adder stone. A stone with a hole in it.'

'No, nothing like that.' The confusion was obvious in Eira's voice. 'The route was obvious.'

Ysolda did not press her. The girl must be lying, but she could not care much why.

'Anyway, I was waiting to see if she came back.'

'Who?'

'Keep up! The Anchorite. But instead I saw you and my mother, then Thane Boreal and that whelp.' She jerked her head at Sami. 'Who is he?'

'He works in the castle. Don't you recognise him?'

'Lots of people work in the castle,' replied Eira. 'Anyway, I guessed it wouldn't end well for you. And that stick, you can read it, can't you?'

There was no point lying. 'Yes.'

'And?'

'I'll tell you if you give me back my amulet.'

Eira rolled her eyes. 'Fine. It's useless anyway.'

She passed it to Ysolda, whose relief caused in her a wave of sickness. She held the amber a moment, the familiar smoothness warmed by Eira's skin. Tears prickled in her eyes as she placed it around her neck. As it clinked against the hag stone, a thought arose. Could the amber have acted as a sort of hag stone for Eira, showing her the safe path across the bog moor? If it had, the girl clearly hadn't guessed.

'Well?' said Eira. 'What's it say?'

'I need to go home,' said Ysolda, dazed. 'The amulet – it needs to be in Glaw Wood.'

'We had a deal,' said the girl.

Impatiently, Ysolda held the stick close to her face to better read it. 'It says: *Not safe. To the high place.*'

'High place,' repeated Eira, and then let out a whoop that made Ysolda jump and Sami start in the canoe so that it rocked side to side.

'Hey!' he shouted.

'I knew it!' said Eira. 'I am a genius, unrivalled among all!'

Ysolda ground her teeth. She was insufferable. 'What does it mean?'

'It means,' said Eira, adjusting their course, 'I know where the Anchorite is. And I'm the only one who does.'

Mention of the ancient girl reminded Ysolda of Thane Boreal's threat. 'We have to go home. To my home.'

'Are you mad?' said Eira. 'It's further away than where we are going.'

'Boreal is going to destroy it. I have to warn them.'

Eira was quiet a moment, and when she spoke again her voice was soft. 'Ysolda, I'm sorry. We wouldn't catch them.

And you saw what Boreal is capable of.'

Panic bloomed in Ysolda's chest. 'I have to go back!'

Nara nuzzled her head, beak sharp in her hair, and Eira reached behind her, catching Ysolda's wrist. She squeezed, and then stroked it with unexpected tenderness. 'I'm sorry. There's nothing there for you now. They're possessed by the need to find her. It's like I told you when we met – finding the Anchorite is our only hope of any power here.'

'My sister,' said Ysolda, holding the amulet with her free hand, 'she's still in the castle.'

'It's secure, she'll be safe.'

'Your mother said she'd free her if we found the Anchorite.'

'There you are then.' Eira released her wrist. 'We know where she is. We can still save your sister.'

Ysolda considered, gripping the amulet tighter. She thought of the many miles she'd travelled, the dangers and the distance. How would she make it back in time? Glaw Wood – she couldn't think about it. But Hari, she could still help Hari.

Though every instinct screamed at her, she knew she had no influence here. 'You swear? If we find her—'

'*When* we find her—'

'We'll go back? We'll rescue Hari?'

'You have my word.' Eira spat on her palm, and held it over her shoulder.

'What are you doing?'

'Isn't that a Glaw Wood thing? No? Well, good – it's gross.' Eira leaned sideways and rinsed her palm in the sea.

'What does it mean then, *to the high place*?'

'The Drakken Peaks, of course,' said Eira. 'High Place is what they were called before the Norse renamed them. The highest mountains in the world.'

'But they're a world away!'

'Not as far as you think.' She nodded at the horizon. 'In Norveger. It is not so far from these islands. Ravi will get us there safely, won't you, boy?'

The wolf barked in reply, and Sami exclaimed as his tail wagged, splashing the canoe.

'Have you ever climbed a mountain?' said Ysolda.

'No. But then, I'd never walked the width of the Isles before, and I'll wager you'd never rode a wolf before you met my mother. All things are possible, even for someone like you.'

Ysolda looked once more behind them. The End-World Wood was a smudge of smoke and flame, the violence made watchable by distance. Somewhere, many miles beyond the burning island, through a felled forest and the Lakes, Hari waited beneath the castle of broken boats, unaware of what was about to befall her beloved home.

Ysolda faced ahead. There was sea, and more sea. And somewhere – at last she truly believed it – an ancient girl with answers so important two rulers were ripping their realms apart to find her. Beneath her chest bone, a small bud of curiosity opened. A tendril of determination.

'All right,' she said. 'We'll find the Anchorite, and then we will save my sister.'

'And more, Glaw Wood girl,' said Eira, a smile in her voice. A hint of the same recklessness her mother shared. 'We'll save the world.'

The ancient forest burned in their wake, but Ysolda did not look back again. On they swam, two girls on a wolf and a boy in a boat, towards the far-off promise of new and perilous lands.

Read on for the first chapter in the next
GEOMANCER book . . .

THE
STORM
AND THE
SEA HAWK

BLACK SHORE

'Land!'

Stars were out above them by the time Ysolda was jerked awake by Eira's shout. As they'd left behind the burning End-World Wood and entered the open ocean, darkness fell fast and a huge fear gripped her, of what was below them, what was behind and in front. She'd squeezed her eyes shut for what she thought was a moment, her hawk Nara chirruping lightly on her shoulder, and woke to true night.

Her mind tried to catch up to where she was: on a swimming wolf's back, in the sea, clutching tight to the wolf queen's daughter. The wolf queen's daughter who was pinching her to wake her fully.

'Ouch!' She pinched Eira back.

'Land!'

'I heard you the first time,' she said blearily, squinting ahead. 'Where?'

'There, *buddhoo*.'

'Don't call me that.' Then, after a pause, 'What's *buddhoo*?'

'What you are.'

Ysolda pinched Eira's side again and the girl kicked water at her. Nara gave a grumpy cry, taking off from Ysolda's shoulder, and a grunt came from the canoe behind as Sami was dashed with freezing seawater.

'Sorry,' said Ysolda, twisting to grimace apologetically at the escaped servant. He was pinched and miserable-looking, huddled in the red cloak in the hollowed-out trunk.

'Forgot you were there,' said Eira on a yawn, leaning forward to stroke Ravi's muzzle. The wolf whined happily, clearly in his element despite the long crossing to Norveger. Sami glowered at her back, and though Ysolda mouthed *sorry* again he turned his glare on her too.

She supposed he had every right to be angry. Even before the journey that had seen him be injured in a fight between the wolf queen and Thane Boreal's warriors, captured by Thane Boreal's Kaltis and nearly burned to death in the End-World Wood, he had been worked to exhaustion in the wolf queen's court. Of course he'd dislike her daughter too.

Ysolda looked over Eira's shoulder to where the coast of

Norveger should be. She still couldn't separate sea-dark from ground-dark, and instead tipped her head back to the sky.

It was domed and huge overhead, Nara swooping, stars poking through celestial dust in their familiar patterns: crab, bear, sword. She couldn't remember ever seeing a night so huge, so bright. She thought of her sister Hari, stuck in the prison below Seren's castle of broken boats, only the occasional shine of fool's gold set in the cave walls for light, the mineral left there to weaken her listening gift.

She tightened her grasp on the amber amulet around her neck, cared for by her sister and now, by mistake and mischance, in her possession once more. Next to it hung the hag stone, gifted to her by Kore, the Forgiver, *to help you see more clearly.* And it had guided her well already, helping her lead the wolf queen across the bog, though Ysolda already regretted that decision.

She had not gone more than a few hours without Hari before, never thought she would be so far away in place and time. What would her sister think if she could see her now, nearing the Norveger coast on wolfback, a Lakes servant in a boat behind and the wolf queen's daughter in front?

She'd probably feel about as happy about it as Ysolda did herself.

She wrapped her arms around her chest, teeth chattering, and wished she hadn't given the red Ryder's cloak to Sami.

'Cold?' asked Eira.

'N-n-no.'

She could almost feel the girl roll her eyes as she said, 'Take my cloak. You drooled all over it while you were asleep anyway. We're nearly there.'

Ysolda unclasped the cloak and pulled the warm wool up under her chin, trying not to breathe in the smell of fabric that had been travelled and slept in by a runaway for weeks.

Now she could start to make out the coast: a jagged line of mountains rising seemingly sheer from the sea. *High Place.* She felt in her pocket for the stick Eira had found in the Anchorite's nest. It was too dark to make out the Ogham message engraved upon it, but Ysolda traced the grooves with her finger. Had the ancient girl really whittled this? And if she had, it meant she spoke Ogham – the language of the trees and of Ysolda's own home, Glaw Wood.

She huffed out her breath, made smoke by the cold air. The season was no longer turning, but turned. The position of the stars told her Mabon was passed, probably while she rode across the Kalti Forest with the wolf queen. The festival of Mabon was her favourite in the forest, made to mark this last burst into colour and plenty as herbs were cropped to be dried and apples picked to be stored in barrels for the winter. In Glaw Wood, they would offer cider to the Elder Alder by pouring it on to its ancient roots, light fires in the clearing beneath its strong branches and dance as the firelight licked the leaves, tingeing them orange as they would become in coming weeks.

But would they, this year? Even before the Ryders came and stole Hari, so much was not the same in her beloved wood. The apples were scarcer, smaller, more bitter. There were fewer traders bringing fish to their cove: Ysolda hadn't seen even their favourite merchant, Finn, for months. The rain was constant – no change there – but brought with it frosts even in the warmer seasons that stretched between Beltane to Litha. They had been small changes, but now Ysolda looked back, they amounted to something odd and wrong.

Happenings, the wolf queen Seren called them. The quake that swallowed Ysolda and Hari's home, the red storm that chased them into shelter. The murderous trees of the Kalti Forest. And other strange things – the lack of birds, of any animals but the fish in Mirror Lake and the gulls that swarmed the castle of broken boats.

Happenings. Warnings. But of what?

Most of what Hari's fellow captor Uncle had told Ysolda was lost to her memory, but she did remember this:

Most realms have their stories about these lines that cross the earth, the language the world speaks across them like voice lines – but of course it is not a language of words. Some call it music, or song. There are many products of these lines. The Anchorite is one of its wonders, the Sea Henge a second, the Drakken Peaks a third, the Hell Gate another. There runs the spirit of the earth, and that is a powerful thing. It allows the world to speak, to sing, to hum across its million million miles and, if needed, to restore balance.

Earth music. Did Ysolda believe such a thing? She was used to Glaw Wood and its certainties, but if she'd learned anything the past days, it was that what she did not know dwarfed what she did.

'Look at that,' said Eira, an unfamiliar note of amazement in her voice. Ysolda peered around her. The peaks were huge and impressive, so large as to feel almost unreal, but most strange was what greeted them on the beach. 'Black sand.'

A long, jagged cove of darkness was enveloping them. Ravi stopped swimming and began wading as the sea floor rose to meet him, whining slightly as his tired legs took their full weight once more. Eira leaped deftly into the shallows, and walked head to shoulder with him, murmuring encouragement as he pulled the canoe on to the shore. Once they were clear of the freezing sea, the wolf slumped on to the black sand and Ysolda slid off his back, numb knees hitting the beach. She felt the grains stick to her hands and wet legs, coarser than she was used to on Glaw Wood's fine golden coast, and as black as obsidian.

'Why is it like that?' Sami's voice was trembling. Ysolda could make out the whites of his eyes as he peered out from his borrowed cloak. 'Is it burned?'

'Sand turns to glass when it burns,' said Eira.

'There are dragons here though,' said Sami.

Eira scoffed. 'Don't be so foolish. There are fire mountains that ignorant people believe hold dragons, but it's only the melting of the earth.'

That sounded terrifying enough to Ysolda. 'Why is it black then?'

'Because the rock is black, see?' Eira pointed at the shadowy peaks looming impossibly high above them. 'The sea grinds them to sand.'

'Water can't break rock,' said Sami.

'Of course it can,' said Eira, 'given time.'

Ysolda was glad it was dark. She wouldn't want Eira to see her expression: a little scared, a little awed at all the wolf queen's daughter knew.

'I still think there might be dragons,' mumbled Sami, climbing clumsily from the canoe, hitting his cramped legs to bring blood back to them.

'You'd better hope not,' said Eira, mischief in her voice glinting as bright as her teeth. 'I heard their favourite meal is servant-boy.'

'Stop that,' snapped Ysolda. She would not let Eira bully Sami. They were not a princess and a servant now, only castaways fleeing from the same woman: the wolf queen, Seren.

'Aren't you gifted?' said Eira, ignoring her and eyeing Sami. 'Can't you summon us a fire or something?'

'I'm a weather weaver,' he mumbled.

'Even better!' Eira rubbed her hands together. 'You can warm us up a bit, get a bit of cloud cover going.'

Sami said something to his feet.

'What?' said Eira impatiently.

'Cold weather,' repeated Sami, louder. 'I can summon cold weather.'

Eira snorted. 'Some gift.'

'Eira!' Ysolda turned sternly to her. 'What now, if you know so much?'

'Now we light a fire seeing as our gifted boy is about as much use as a wet cloak right now.'

'Enough!'

Eira huffed. 'Then we can get Ravi dry and let him rest.' She threw herself down in the sand next to the panting wolf.

'We should collect some firewood then,' said Ysolda, getting achingly to her feet.

'Yes,' said Eira, flinging an arm across her eyes and waving her away with her other hand, yawning widely. '*We* should.'

Dear Reader,

You hold in your hands the book I've wanted to write since I realised I wanted to write at all. A whole-hearted, action-packed trilogy, built on real-world foundations. Across three books, you'll experience a war between queens, thanes, and the earth beneath their feet. *In the Shadow of the Wolf Queen* is just the start, in more ways than one.

This story is rooted in the real, the elemental. Its first glimmers came to me as I walked in the Celtic Rainforests in Eryri, North Wales, a micro climate unique to the area. So much green: moss, leaves, the algae of the river. The smell itself was green and alive. It was a moment of true connection to nature, a noticing moment. So when I began dreaming the Geomancer trilogy into existence, I knew I wanted it to be a celebration of what the world could and does do.

I'm a fierce believer in the power of stories, and this is a celebration of the storytelling traditions of my childhood – a mixture of Welsh, Indian, Viking and eastern European heritage means I was raised with the most imaginative, varied and thrilling myths. I wanted my characters to reflect the incredible range of experience and cultures I've seen within my own family, and ask what that world would look like, taste like, sound like.

Everywhere in this book is based on a real place in the United Kingdom, renamed the Isles. Glaw Wood is based on the Celtic Rainforests that first inspired me. The Lakes are the Lake District, the Kalti Forest, the Scottish pinewoods. The End-World Wood, where Ysolda seeks a girl more myth than flesh, is Stroma Island. As her adventure grows over the next two books, so does the map, and I look forward to taking you to more astounding places. I have plumbed the depths of what is possible, what is happening, and what could happen, to force Ysolda into dangers that are not only present, but provable.

What I hope you are left with is a sense of how astonishing nature is, and how the world needs fewer heroes and more ordinary people, showing extraordinary care.

Kiran Millwood Hargrave
Oxford, 2023

Want to learn more about the secret lives of trees?
Visit woodlandtrust.org.uk to find woodland near you, find
out facts about forests, and even watch an osprey nest live
on camera during nesting season. For specific information
about the Celtic Rainforest and its conservation,
visit celticrainforests.wales.

Acknowledgements

First thank you always to my mother Andrea, the woman who taught me strength and ferocity, and how love is the basis of both. My father Martyn, for gifting me curiosity and unlocking the secrets of wood, sea, and stone. My brother John, a healer and a hiker, who is at his happiest on an adventure. My grandparents, Yvonne and John, still walking the Norfolk coast and naming the birds, reading the tides, showing me so much beauty so close to home. More than ever, my grandparents Carol and Raj, Laura and Fred, kept alive in my family's mouths and in our faces. My aunts and uncles, from India, Bangladesh, Yorkshire, Poland, and

Canada, telling me stories from around the world. My cousins, here and remembered, my in-laws and my niblings, growing my wonder and my heart beyond imagining.

My agent Hellie Ogden, for clearing the path and pulling me onwards. The Janklow and Nesbit team for their belief and support. My editors Rachel Wade and Nazima Abdillahi – I'm so grateful we are working on Ysolda's tale together. Thank you for your guidance and wisdom. Designer Alison Padley, always integral to the vision and the excitement. Manuel Šumberac, for the stunning illustrations. My publicist Emily Thomas, working on the grand and the granular. The Geomancer team at Hachette: Naomi Berwin, Fiona Evans, Beth McWilliams, Annabel El-Kerim, the wider rights, publicity and marketing teams working so passionately to bring this book to readers.

To Georgina Kamsika, sense and sensitivity reader! Thank you for your generous insight and encouragement, which so shaped this story. To Fiona Noble, for your early support. To Florentyna Martin, without whom so much wouldn't have been possible.

I feel blessed to be friends with some of my favourite storytellers, especially Katie Webber, Kevin Tsang, Katherine Rundell, Anna James, Krystal Sutherland, Robin Stevens, Ella Risbridger, Samantha Shannon, Alwyn Hamilton, Cat Doyle, Sophie Anderson, Jessie Burton, Piers Torday, Cressida Cowell, Martin Stewart, Katya Balen, Ross Montgomery, Sam Sedgeman, M.G. Leonard, Varsha Shah, Maz Evans, Lizzie Huxley-Jones, Melinda Salisbury, Sita Brahmachari, and Frances Hardinge. Your stories have inspired my own, and illuminated my life.

To Sarvat Hasin and Daisy Johnson – I would not, could not, write or function without you. To the Unruly Writers, especially Samir Guglani, Rory Gleeson, and Agnes Davis, amongst whom I first found my voice. To my dear friends Jess Patterson, Hatty Martin, Jess Oliver, Izzy Penney, who are always there for the ups and downs.

To booksellers, librarians, teachers, and readers. This story is yours now.

To my husband, Tom de Freston, who walks beside me always, even when I can't see the wood for the trees. To Coral, a longed-for spark that has become our sun, the light and centre of our lives.

KIRAN MILWOOD HARGRAVE is an award-winning,
bestselling novelist. Her debut story for children,
The Girl of Ink & Stars, won the Waterstones Children's Book
Prize, and the British Book Awards Children's Book of the Year.
Her work has been short- and long-listed for numerous major
prizes including the Costa Award and the Carnegie Award, and
her novel *Julia and the Shark*, illustrated by Tom de Freston,
was shortlisted for the Wainwright Prize and named Waterstones
Children's Gift of the Year. She's a graduate of both Oxford and
Cambridge Universities, and lives in Oxford with her husband,
daughter and cats, in a house between a
river and a forest.

26/7/24.

Look out for the second
GEOMANCER BOOK

THE
STORM
AND THE
SEA HAWK